CURVEBALL
The Year I Lost My Grip

also by Jordan Sonnenblick

Drums, Girls & Dangerous Pie

Notes from the Midnight Driver

Zen and the Art of Faking It

After Ever After

CURVEBALL
The Year I Lost My Grip

JORDAN SONNENBLICK

SCHOLASTIC INC.

This book was originally published in hardcover by Scholastic Press in 2012.

ISBN 978-0-545-32070-2

12 11 10 9 8 7 6 5 4 3 2 1   14 15 16 17 18 19/0

Printed in the U.S.A.   40
This edition first printing, January 2014

The text type was set in Gill Sans.
Book design by Elizabeth B. Parisi

In memory of two great teachers: DENIS KIELY and FRANK McCOURT. You told me I had stories to tell, and made me believe it.

acknowledgments

Three amazing local experts in Pennsylvania helped me with the research for this book: Laurie J. Goodrich, Senior Monitoring Biologist at Hawk Mountain Sanctuary; Brian Pepe, MSPAS, PA-C.A.T., C, Physician Assistant at Children's HealthCare, Allentown; and Steven B. Miller, Jr., at Dan's Camera City, Allentown, who is without a doubt the most patient camera salesman in the universe.

I also learned a lot from two extraordinary educators at Phillipsburg High School in New Jersey, along with their students. Thanks to teachers Andy Herbster and Lisa Weindel for showing me the ropes of high school journalism. Thanks, too, to students Kaley Beesley, Sam Lavin, Terese Yale, and Max Daigle for walking me through what yearbook and newspaper editors and photographers actually edit and photograph.

I got a ton of information from each of these people, although any errors of fact or interpretation are purely my own.

table of contents

"Oop! The Moment!

Once you miss it, it is gone forever!"

HENRI CARTIER-BRESSON,

legendary photographer

CURVEBALL
The Year I Lost My Grip

when i was little . . .

The very first thing I can remember is this: I am really, really mad at my mom for some reason. I'm sitting in the middle of the living room, arms crossed, pouting. At this stage, I am a world-champion pouter. There's an old guy — my grandfather — kneeling in front of me, trying to cheer me up.

"Come on!" he says. "If you give me just one smile, I promise I'll . . . umm . . . I'll give you a mint!"

I remember thinking, *A mint? He thinks I'm going to give in completely, just to get a mint?*

When I don't smile, or even uncross my stubby little arms, he ups the offer. "OK, what if I buy you an ice cream?"

Ice cream, huh? Now he's talking my language. But I'm still mad, so I shake my head and concentrate on pouting harder.

Grampa leans in really close and whispers, "Peter, what if I give you a tour of my studio?"

This is too good to be true. Grampa is a professional photographer, and he never lets me go into his studio. Whenever I ask, he tells me, "You don't want to go in there. You wouldn't be allowed to touch anything. Besides, it smells like chemicals from the darkroom." But that only makes me want to go in there even more. It's Grampa's Special Place, where he goes to Make Art. And Money!

Still, even at age three or whatever, I know how to play it cool. "I don't know," I say. "Can I go to your studio *and* get a mint? That way, I won't even smell the menicals. . . ."

Grampa looks puzzled for a second, then laughs. "Menicals? You mean chemicals! All right, big man. Let's see that smile!"

I smile, big-time. Grampa takes my hands, walks outside with me, and puts me in his Big Truck, an SUV with a big yellow picture of a mountain on the side. In classy-looking letters I can't read yet, the words GOLDBERG PHOTO are printed right under the back window. We drive across town to the studio.

I have no idea how long we spent in the studio that day, partly because I've spent so much time there since then that I can't be one hundred percent sure which memories are which. But I remember being in awe. Huge blowups of Grampa's photos are everywhere. There is a whole wall of brides: My grampa gets to look at a *lot* of beautiful ladies. Another wall is just for landscapes: The sun rising over the Alps. A pond with mist hanging over it. A desert that seems to stretch into infinity. My grampa gets to go to all of these places! The third wall is the best of all, even though it's kind of scary, too. Everywhere I look, there's something shocking: Soldiers, with real guns! An angry tiger, looking right at me! A cobra, raised up to strike! My grampa has looked at all of these dangerous things, with nothing but a camera between him and them.

Clearly, Grampa is the coolest person in the world. "Well," he says, after I have gaped at every photo, "these pictures are my life's work. Do you like them?"

I nod really hard. Grampa grins and asks, "Do you have any questions?"

I look at the pictures some more. I have been wondering something the whole time, trying to imagine my grampa looking through his camera lens and pushing the button to take each of the pictures, but I am having trouble expressing it as a question. Fortunately, Grampa is amazing at waiting. Eventually, I blurt, "How do you *know*?"

"How do I know what?"

"How do you know the picture is going to be so good? Right when you push the button. How do you know?"

He laughs again. "Well, first of all, sometimes I take bad pictures, too. Only I don't blow them up and frame them for everybody to see. But . . . when a shot is going to be really, really good, you can just tell."

"How? *How*, Grampa?" I want to know, because I want to take pictures exactly like these someday.

Grampa looks thoughtful for a while, not saying anything. Then he bends his knees so we are eye to eye, puts his hand on my shoulder, and says, "I don't know, pal. Sometimes, you just know it when you see it."

Snap 1

The first picture is a wide-angle shot, taken through the chain-link fence of the backstop behind home plate. There's a boy standing on a pitcher's mound in full uniform: green and gold. His cap is pulled low over his eyes, and his unruly black hair sticks out below the brim in all directions. He leans in toward home plate, his throwing arm dangling loose at his side. He must be looking in to get his sign from the catcher.

The second picture is zoomed in a lot closer, a full-body shot of the pitcher alone. He's standing sideways now, but his head is turned toward the plate, and you can tell he is about a thousandth of a second away from going into his windup. Maybe because he's fully upright, or maybe because of the tighter shot, you can just make out his eyes in this one. The look on his face is intense, like he is trying to stare a laser line right through the batter, the catcher, the umpire, even the photographer. The pitcher might be concentrating really, really hard. Or he might be in a whole lot of pain. It's hard to tell.

The next several photos are taken all in a row, click, click-click. Each is zoomed in more tightly than the one before it. The pitcher is in his windup, one arm cocked behind his head, his glove hand swinging down, across his body, toward the catcher. Then the throwing arm is whipping its way forward in stop-time as his compact body is launched forward by the thrust of his back leg against the pitching rubber. There's a shot that freezes the action just as the ball leaves the pitcher's hand. His arm is coming straight down, and his entire body is tumbling forward. If you look past all of the moving limbs, you might be able to tell that something has gone wrong. The pitcher's face is now stretched in a grimace of agony.

In the next shot, the pitcher has fallen halfway out of the frame so that you can only see his head, his shoulders, a blur of infield, outfield, the blue sky. The photographer adjusts in a split second, swinging the camera downward just enough to center his subject in the frame one more time. Now the pitcher has tumbled to his knees, and his glove hand is pressed against the elbow of his throwing arm. Click. There's another photo, blurred as though the photographer is moving when the shutter opens: the boy falling forward. You can tell his face is going to hit the dirt at the foot of the pitcher's mound. You can tell it's probably going to hurt.

The photographer is my grandfather.

The pitcher is me.

1. click

If I had known it was going to be the last baseball game I'd ever play, I would have asked my mom to bring the video camera or something. But you never know that kind of stuff in advance. All you can do is play every game like it's your final shot at the World Series, and hope that for you, it isn't.

It was the summer after eighth grade. I was the relief pitcher, trying to close out a 2–1 victory in the league championship. All I needed to do was get through one inning without giving up a run. My best friend, AJ Moore, was catching, as usual. We were the two best pitchers on the team. Actually, we were the two best pitchers in the league, and the two best catchers — which meant that when I pitched, he caught, and vice versa. It was a unique situation, having two best friends pitching to each other all the time. I mean, really unique, the kind of unique that gets written up in the newspaper. The kind of unique that makes the town's high school baseball coach come out to scout our post-season games.

The kind of unique that girls notice. AJ and I were the golden boys of eighth grade. He actually was a golden boy: almost six feet tall, with blond hair, bright blue eyes, and a relaxed smoothness that came from knowing everyone loved him. I wasn't literally quite as golden. As in, I was a five-foot-three Jewish kid with black hair, pale skin, and glasses. AJ was a power-throwing righty; I was a sneaky, deceptive lefty. AJ was a natural catcher. I had to work my butt off behind the plate, which was made harder by the fact that I was the only lefty catcher at our level in the whole league. Generally, coaches frown on left-handed kids becoming catchers, so you have to be really, really good at it if you ever want to get any playing time at the position.

Off the field, the differences between us were just as obvious. Where AJ was smooth, I was prickly. He smiled, I brooded. He could laugh things off, but I took everything too seriously. He liked winning, but I lived to win. When we lost, he would scowl at the time but get over it when he left the field. I would go home and punch my pillow for half an hour. Fortunately, I had two things going for me that helped my social standing: I was an athlete, and I was AJ's friend.

Anyway, the way things were supposed to go in this game was that I would blow away the first three batters I faced, in order, and we would win the Lehigh Valley Knee-High Baseball League title for the second year in a row. The high school coach would be so impressed with AJ and me that he would make us starting pitchers on the JV team when we got to ninth grade. AJ had pitched six great innings to get us this far, and now I was on the mound. All I had to do was the usual.

I tried to ignore the stabbing ache in my left elbow. That pain, which had been with me all season, was my biggest secret. Nobody knew about it, and I mean nobody. Not AJ, not any of my coaches, and certainly not my parents. If the coaches knew, they might not let me pitch. And if my parents found out, forget about it. They would absolutely freak. Mom would rush onto the field and be all like "My baby! MY BA-A-A-BY!" Then I would basically have to move to Canada.

Ever since AJ's massive growth spurt in seventh grade had left me a whole head shorter than he was, I had been overthrowing the ball. I knew it, but that was the only way I was going to compete, keep getting batters out, and — hopefully — make the high school team. So I would throw fastball after fastball until it felt like my elbow was getting mashed up in a meat grinder, and then I'd mix in a couple of curveballs, which felt even worse. On the other hand, at this point I figured I was only nine good pitches — three strikeouts — away from a whole winter of rest and recovery.

Nine. Freaking. Good. Pitches.

The first batter was easy. AJ had gotten him out twice with nothing but fastballs, so I figured he would jump all over my first pitch. AJ signaled for a changeup, and the guy pounded the ball straight into the ground. It rolled about three feet in front of the plate. AJ pounced on the ball and whipped it to first. One away.

Batter Number Two was no problem. AJ hadn't shown him anything but fastballs, either. I had a feeling he'd lay off the first pitch after what I had just done to the leadoff dude, and I was right. I threw a change right in there for a strike. I knew he'd jump on the second pitch. AJ signaled for another change, down in the dirt. I missed my spot completely and threw it high. Luckily, the kid swatted at the ball, and hit a soft pop-up to third base.

The third batter stepped into the box: their first baseman. A hard-hitting lefty who had already hit two doubles off of AJ. I figured that was all right. Lefties have trouble hitting left-handed pitching. All I had to do was get one fastball by him. Then I could throw a curveball right at his head. He would flinch, but the ball would break down and away from him, and hopefully end up on the inside corner of the strike zone. Follow that with an inside changeup, and I'd be done.

AJ put down one finger in the classic catcher's sign for a fastball. I took a deep breath, wound up, and hurled the ball as hard as I could. Something clicked in my elbow joint, like there were two pennies snapping past each other in there. It took every ounce of determination I had not to grab my arm and whimper. The batter hit a screaming liner down the left-field line, maybe three feet foul.

Wow, this kid had fast hands.

AJ put down one finger again. I shook my head: There was no way I was going to get another fastball past this kid. Even if my arm didn't explode in the process, I just couldn't throw hard enough. AJ trotted out to me, put an arm around my shoulder, and muttered, "What's going on, Peter?"

"Nothing. I just don't think I can get another fastball by him."

"Dude, I'm telling you, this kid killed my off-speed stuff. You have to bring the fastball."

"AJ, I can't."

"What do you mean, you can't?"

I just looked at him. "You're hurt, aren't you?" he asked.

I looked away. "It's fine," I said. From the corner of my eye, I saw the home-plate umpire stand up straight and start heading toward the mound. It looked like meeting time was over.

AJ sighed. "All right, Pete. Curveball in?"

I stared right into AJ's eyes, trying to thank him without thanking him. "Curveball in." AJ trotted back behind home plate, the ump got settled into his crouch and pointed his finger at me — the "Play ball!" signal — and I toed the pitching rubber. It was time for business.

The curveball felt very nearly as bad as the fastball had, with that same horrible bony click in my elbow. But the batter flinched and whiffed. Then I threw the inside changeup exactly where I wanted it.

Unfortunately, the guy didn't swing. One ball, two strikes. And I didn't have anything left to throw at him. AJ put down the changeup sign again, but I knew the kid wouldn't swing at a change unless I put it right down the middle of the plate. I shook my head. AJ put down the fastball sign — what choice did he have? I shrugged him off yet again. He looked at me. I looked at him. Clearly, we had both done the math. There was nothing left but the curve.

AJ jogged out to me again. This time, our coach came out of the dugout. Coach got to me first. "Whaddaya doin', Petey? Give 'im the fastball. Let's win this thing and go get some pizza." AJ started to say something, but Coach silenced him with a glare. I nodded. Sometimes in life, even when you know it's going to hurt, you just have to throw that fastball.

While Coach walked back to the bench, and AJ got himself set up again, I took a little stroll to the back of the mound. I bent over, picked up the rosin bag, and tossed it up and down a couple of times. My knees were a little shaky. My arm throbbed worse than it had ever throbbed before. I took a deep breath, dropped the bag, stepped up to the rubber, and tried to tell myself positive thoughts: *It's only one more pitch. How bad can it be? You can be a hero or you can be a wuss. And Peter Friedman is no wuss.*

The batter stepped into the box. The ump pointed to me. AJ got his glove down around the outside corner of the strike zone. I went into my windup. As my hand turned behind my left ear, I felt another of those strange penny clicks. I gasped, closed my eyes for a split second, and whipped my arm forward as hard as I could. Maybe a thousandth of a second after the ball left my hand, my elbow locked up completely. I fell to my knees in front of the mound. As bad as the pain had been before, this was a whole new experience. I saw lights flashing in front of my eyes. *Don't cry*, I told myself. *You are on the field in the middle of a game. You. Will. Not. Cry.*

I tried to look around and figure out what had happened with the pitch, but things were starting to get blurry. Also, I noticed I wasn't on my knees anymore. Somehow, I had fallen all the way forward, and there was cool dirt against my right cheek. I had the feeling people were talking. They might even have been shouting. But it all kind of sounded like underwater music or something. Then hands were on me.

AJ said, "Pete! Pete! Can you hear me?"

I was afraid that if I talked, my voice would have that crying sound to it, and everyone would know I was weak. But I was even more afraid someone might try to move my elbow. "It's my arm. Don't move my arm!"

Then Coach was kneeling next to me. I forgot about the arm for a second. "Did I get him?" I muttered. "Is it over?"

"You did great, Pete. It's all over. Now I'm just going to try and sit you up, all right? AJ, support his head. Ready? One, two, three . . ."

They rolled me up and over, and the whole world spun like I had just gotten off the mother of all roller coasters. Now I was on my butt in the grass in front of the mound, facing first base. The batter was standing on the bag. I whirled back around to face Coach. "Wait, I thought I got him," I said. Now my voice was starting to tear up. I saw Coach gesturing to our dugout, and noticed that the assistant coach was on his way up the steps with a first-aid kit. My parents and grandfather were all right there, too, leaning against the chain-link fence, looking painfully scared.

Coach said, "Pete, I'm going to move your arm around a little bit, OK? Just tell me where it hurts."

I wanted to shout, "No-o-o-o-o!!" but I knew I was about a half second away from bawling my eyes out, and now the entire team was standing in a semi-circle around me. Coach took my hand and rolled my wrist maybe half an inch.

I heard a strangled, high-pitched scream. I wondered where it was coming from for an instant, until I realized my mouth was wide open. Everything started going black around the edges, and I was slumping over again. The last thing I remember seeing was that hitter, standing on first base like he owned it.

2. Shooting eagles

One day later that summer, six weeks after my elbow surgery, my grandfather picked me up before dawn on a surprisingly cold and windy Saturday to go on a little photo safari. For years, we had gone hiking together with cameras pretty often. When I wasn't playing sports, you could usually find us together snapping pictures of nature scenes, old-fashioned trains, or whatever else Grampa thought I might like — but this day was different. Grampa wouldn't tell me where we were going, or even how long we would be gone.

I mean, I didn't care. All I had been doing for weeks was sit around the house, watch sports, eat Cheetos, and complain. Except when I was at physical therapy, where I would sweat, grunt, and complain. My parents kept trying to find stuff for me to do, but the only things I was even remotely interested in doing were things I could never, ever do again. I mean, I was supposed to be in my seventh summer of baseball camp for the whole month of July, and my fifth summer of basketball academy for most of August.

But when you're not allowed to go anywhere near a ball, it's kinda hard to get your money's worth out of sports camp. So that's how I found myself trudging along in the dark behind Grampa, schlepping a heavy backpack full of camera equipment up the side of a mountain somewhere in the Pennsylvania stretch of the Appalachian Trail. Aside from the backpack, I also carried a tripod in my good hand. Grampa was carrying a camera bag, plus a separate canvas knapsack full of sandwiches, drinks, and whatever other provisions my mother had thoughtfully forced him to lug uphill. Mom meant well, but I was pretty sure she believed I would starve if I spent three hours in the woods without a gajillion calories of snacks on hand.

Grampa led me through woods, over areas of broken rock, into and out of moss-covered clearings, and finally out into the open. I gasped. We were basically at the top of a cliff. There was a field of gigantic boulders, and then ... nothing. Grampa picked his way carefully over several of the rocks, and I followed. Now we were right near the edge, looking out over a deep valley. Actually, it was almost a canyon. The sun was coming up, but we were facing north, so it was still pretty dark below us.

Grampa gestured for the camera bag and tripod, and without speaking, I started helping him set up. I still didn't know why we had to be on a cliff this early to take whatever pictures he wanted, but I had been helping Grampa shoot pictures for what felt like forever, so I knew the general drill. For the next few minutes, Grampa gave instructions. Grampa was never big on talking about anything but photography when he was getting ready to shoot. He did this for a living, and he never messed around when there was a camera in his hand.

"Peter, get me the Nikon with the two-point-eight telephoto lens. No, the longer one — the four hundred."

Wow, that was a serious lens. I mean, a couple thousand bucks worth of serious. Long zooms are expensive, and lenses that let in a lot of light are expensive. Lenses that are long and bright — forget about it. I was kind of nervous about putting something that valuable on a shaky tripod . . . on a boulder . . . on the edge of a cliff. I raised one eyebrow, and Grampa said, "What?"

"Uh, nothing. I just . . . I mean, I'm wondering what the heck we're going to be shooting that you need such serious glass for." "Glass" is the generic photographers' term for lenses, especially the really good lenses you put on fancy professional-type cameras. Most of the time, when we went out into the woods to take pictures of deer and snakes and stuff, we could get pretty close to the animals, and the light was good. So why take a chance and bust out with the super-pricey lenses?

Grampa sighed, settled his long body down so that he was sitting on one fairly flat boulder and leaning back against another, and asked me to put the tripod right in front of him. Then he squinted at me in the slanted light that was coming from behind him over the rocks. Between the angle and the way he was silhouetted against the dawn, I couldn't be sure, but I almost thought I saw my grandfather wink.

"Eagles," he said, leaning forward to look through the camera's eyepiece. "We're shooting eagles."

"Eagles? How do you know we're going to see eagles here?"

"Easy. This valley is right along their seasonal migration route. On a good day, something like fifteen eagles fly by this lookout."

"Is this a good day?"

"Could be. It's windy enough. Coffee?" He reached into the backpack I'd been carrying and took out a thermos and two cups. Mom would have totally disapproved of her father giving me coffee, but he'd been doing it for years whenever we went out on our photo missions. When I was a little kid, when Grampa came to pick me up, I would always ask if we were going on a Man's Journey. He would always say, "That's right. I'll be the big man . . ." Then I would say, "And I'll be the *other* big man!" Then I would laugh my head off.

Guess you had to be there.

I sipped my coffee. You'd think a tough old guy like Grampa would drink it black, but actually he loved cream and sugar. It was like having a mug of warm ice cream. We didn't talk for a long time. That might have been the best thing about being with him: You didn't have to think of stuff to say every minute. We could spend three hours together cleaning lenses, or editing photos on the computer, or even just driving in his SUV to some wildlife preserve in the middle of nowhere, and it never felt uncomfortable.

I might have dozed off a little bit, because the next thing I knew, my coffee was cold, the sun was up over the ridgeline, and I had to pee like a bandit. I looked over at Grampa, and he was sitting perfectly still, except for his eyes. His eyes were scanning the sky from left to right, then back again. I stood up and walked down the trail to find an unobtrusive place to urinate.

When I got back, Grampa was fiddling around with the camera. I knew what he was doing, because I would have thought of it, too. Now that the sun was getting higher, he was screwing a polarizing filter on to the end of the lens so that the sky wouldn't look too bright or washed out if an eagle came flying by. "So, Grampa," I said, "have you ever done this before? I mean, you've never taken me here."

He smiled. "I've been coming here at least twice every August for thirty years. Once, when your mom was a kid, I started to get bored of shooting nothing but parties, so I picked the hardest shot I could think of and vowed to get it someday. I mean, people get married all the time, but an eagle coming over the mountain, right at sunrise? That's a once-in-a-lifetime deal . . . a major challenge. You always have to challenge yourself, Pete. Remember that."

"And you always come here alone?"

"Every time."

"Then why —"

"Why are you here, Pete?"

"Well, yeah."

He didn't say anything for the longest time as his eyes flicked back and forth along the horizon. Then I understood. "Mom told you to talk to me."

He nodded.

"About what?"

"Your arm. Your plans. School."

"What are you supposed to be telling me? My arm hurts and I probably can't pitch again. What plans am I supposed to have? And what about school? It will start, and I'll show up every day and go to classes."

Grampa poured himself a refill. He always said that after forty years of shooting weddings, he could stand still in a tux for six hours without a bathroom break, and from what I'd seen, that wasn't an exaggeration. It was like the man had an entire extra bladder hidden away in some other dimension or something. In tense situations, it meant that you would always, always squirm before he did.

"Pete, your mom and dad are both concerned about you. They wanted me to tell you that we're here for you if you need anything." Grampa looked a little bit embarrassed; he wasn't a big emotional-speech kind of guy. "Oh, and . . . well . . . you need to join a club."

"A club? What kind of club?"

"Dunno. Your mom got a brochure from the high school, and it said freshmen are strongly encouraged to participate in after-school activities. So, if you aren't going to be doing sports . . ."

"Great. Maybe I can join the knitting society."

He gave me his devastating Blue-Gray Eyes of Death stare.

"Chess club?"

The eyes were still upon me.

"Irish step dance?"

Grampa sighed. I never could take it when Grampa sighed. "Fine," I said. "Tell her I'll look into it, OK?"

He nodded, ever so slightly, then turned back to searching the sky. Grampa used to have the sharpest vision of anybody in the world, by the way. For the next hour or so, every few minutes I would see a big bird, jump up, and point. Grampa would mutter, "Hawk," and keep looking. Apparently, we weren't there to shoot hawks.

At one point, I asked, "How long are we going to sit here?"

"Why? Got a date?" He smirked.

We waited some more. I took another trailside bathroom break. I paced back and forth across the rocks. I crept forward to take a peek over the edge of the cliff. I took out the spare camera body we always carried, fished around for Grampa's 85mm portrait lens, and started shooting candids of my grandfather from various points among the rocks.

God, I was restless. I swear, I could never shoot weddings. Plus, my left arm was aching. The doctors said it would do that for at least another month, as the cartilage regenerated to replace the piece that had broken loose inside of my elbow joint in the spring. Ugh.

Then Grampa said, "Pete." I looked over, and a huge, amazing bald eagle was flying right toward us.

3. furr-reshmannn!

You have these dreams of what the first day of high school will be like, you know? You'll walk down the hallway and all your boys will give you high fives. Hot girls from the other middle schools will check you out as they whisper and giggle behind their hands. The teachers will immediately notice your incredible brilliance. The coaches will seek you out and invite you to try out for their teams, although they also tell you that, for you, the tryout is just a formality. If you get lost or something, you'll be guided to class by some of the friendly and nurturing upperclassmen.

I'm here to tell you, my introduction to ninth grade wasn't quite that good. First of all, I kept getting jostled and banged around in the halls, so my bad arm (that's how I thought of it now) felt like someone was stirring it around in a vat of ground glass. Second, I got lost over and over again, but nobody came jogging over to rescue me. At one point, I asked a girl who looked like she would know her way around, and she and her friends made a whole big deal out of teasing me:

Ooh, look at the cute little furr-reshmannnnnn! Are you lost, little freshy-guy? Where do you need to go? Don't worry, we won't let you wander the big, scary halls. Will we, ladies? Now, all you have to do is go through this big metal thing called a door, and then walk up these steppy things called the staircase, and . . .

I basically just wanted to die. Especially because the girl was a complete babe, and I could feel my face bursting into a crazy blush. That was on my way to third block, which for me meant my elective art class: Introduction to Photography. We had gotten a course guide in the spring of eighth grade, and when I was looking over it with my parents, my mom had forced me to sign up for this one. I could still hear her voice ringing in my ear half a year later: *Ooh, that will be perfect for you! You know so much about cameras already — it will be an easy A.*

And look — it counts in your grade point average! It's never too early to think about looking good to colleges. . . . I had tried to tell her that photography was a private thing between me and Grampa, but that had gone over like a lead balloon. So not only had I given in, but I had also convinced AJ to sign up with me.

AJ and I met up on the way into class. He asked me how my day had been, but totally stopped listening when this one girl walked in. My back was to the door, so I didn't really see anything except that she was tiny and had on a black hoodie. From my angle, she could have been anybody. Apparently, from his angle, not so much. "Wow," he said. "Cuteness alert! Thanks for making me take this class, Pete. I love you, man!"

Half an hour into the period, I was ready to strangle my mom. First of all, the teacher had stomped into the room and immediately assigned us seats alphabetically — never a good sign — which put me across the room from AJ. Second, Mom and I both should have paid a little more attention to the

"Introduction" part, because the teacher was saying stuff like "The lens is the part of the camera that lets light in." And "One important thing to remember with a digital camera is that water is *not* your friend." Or my favorite: "If you all pass the first three written tests, in just a few short weeks you'll be ready to touch a real camera!"

I snuck a glance over to the far corner of the lab, where AJ was sitting, looking bored out of his skull. He was completely going to kill me for getting him into this. The girl he had pointed out was sitting next to me, and she looked bored out of her mind, too. In fact, she was muttering sarcastic comebacks under her breath, à la "Oh, so the lens cap needs to be *off* for best results! Ooh, better write that one down." I tried to eavesdrop without being obvious about it, but when she said, "A *real* camera? In just a *few short weeks*? Mercy! We're not worthy!" I snorted.

She noticed. More than that: She turned and stared at me. Head-on, she was really pretty, in an angular way. She had jet-black hair that fell long and a little bit wavy over one shoulder, dark wire-rimmed glasses, sharp cheekbones, a tiny nose that might have been slightly pointy, and the palest blue eyes in the world. I mean, incredibly pale blue, like the eyes of a sled dog or something. Which might sound unattractive, but somehow on her, these eyes were working. She would have been cute with regular, normal-colored eyes — but with the ones she had, she was slaying me.

"Don't look at me," she stage-whispered. "You might miss some priceless tidbits."

I just looked at her some more, because I didn't know what to say. Between the eyes and the incredibly rare conversational use of "tidbits," I think I was stunned.

She raised an eyebrow. I felt myself blushing for the second time in less than an hour. "Seriously, dude," she said. "Tidbits."

I kept staring. In a few seconds, this girl was either going to have to marry me, or get a restraining order.

She pointed one finger across her body at the teacher. "Come on! This way to the tidbits!"

That finally did it. I laughed out loud. I mean, *This way to the tidbits?* Who *wouldn't* be forced to laugh? I turned back toward the teacher, who was glaring at me. He had the class list in his hand. This was so not good. "What's your name, young man?"

First the "tidbits," now the "young man." What was this, Outdated Expression Day? "Peter Friedman, sir."

I caught the girl, in the corner of my vision, mouthing, "Sir?"

"Well, Peter Friedman, perhaps you'd like to repeat what I just said about the difference between automatic and manual modes on a digital camera."

Ugh. The old repeat-after-me trick. "Um, did you say that automatic mode figures out the aperture, shutter speed, ISO speed, white balance, flash setting, and —"

He cut me off.

"Mr. Friedman, what do you mean by aperture?"

"Well, it's the width of the opening in the lens."

"And what is ISO speed?"

"That would be, umm, the light sensitivity of the

camera's sensor. If you turn it way down, you get more clarity, but your shutter speed has to be slower and —"

The teacher cut me off again. "What are you doing here, Mr. Friedman?"

"Uh, I'm in this class."

"No, I mean why are you in an introductory photo class when you clearly know a lot about photography already?"

"Well, uh, I thought . . ."

"You thought you'd get an easy A, didn't you? I think we had better send you across the hall to Advanced Photographic Techniques. Grab your things."

Before I even knew what hit me, I was sitting in a different classroom, surrounded by upperclassmen. Wow, AJ was completely going to kill me. I met my new teacher, Mr. Marsh, who had the strongest New York accent I had ever heard. He welcomed me in by saying, "Take any empty chay-uh, Peetuh!" I sat down, looked around, and instantly knew this class was going to be a whole lot more challenging than the one I had just left. There were huge blowup prints of all kinds of photos all around me: nature, sports, portraits. There were also a couple of expensive SLR camera bodies lying around on tables, and a class set of super-new computers with huge monitors. As I found a seat — which wasn't hard because there were only maybe eight people in the class — Mr. Marsh introduced himself and went right back to what he had been doing.

About five minutes later, just as Mr. Marsh was demonstrating how to choose between three different kinds of lens filters (or "filtuhs") for outdoor photography, the door opened again. Blue Eyes Girl walked in.

AJ was absolutely, completely going to kill me.

For the first time all day, I smiled.

4. nightmares

I didn't sleep well the first week of freshman year. I know you're thinking I was probably worried about all the usual new-school stuff: settling into classes and making friends and not getting stuffed into a locker for the weekend by hulking football players. But as scary as those things were, they weren't horrifying enough to make it into my nightmares that week.

No, my dreams were way, way worse than that. They were all pretty much variations on two themes. The first one always featured a flashback of what had happened a few weeks before with my grandfather and the eagle trip: Grampa sitting on the edge of a cliff with his camera and me crouching next to him, looking through the viewfinder of the spare camera. The eagle appeared and I tried to line up a shot. But everything else was a crazed distortion. In real life, I had gotten maybe fifteen shots off, but half of them were blurry and the other half had the eagle at least halfway out of the frame. Grampa hadn't taken a single shot. It was like he was frozen in place, for no apparent reason. When the eagle had gone, I looked over at Grampa, and he was just staring over the ridge blankly. After maybe a minute, he jumped up, shook himself like he was waking up from a day-dream, and started packing. We went home in a weird, stunned silence. Back at the house, Grampa had unpacked all of his camera gear from the back of the SUV, brought it into my room, and said, "Here, Pete, this is all yours now. I'm done." Then he hugged me hard and left. I tried to get him to stop and talk — to tell me what was going on — but he just walked away.

In the dream, just as the bird appeared, Grampa turned to me and his furious face filled my view-screen, blocking the eagle completely. As the focus-indicator lights flashed red, he shouted, "Get the shot! Get the shot! What's wrong with you? Gotta get the goddamn shot, Pete!" Then he leaned in even closer until I turned, dropped the camera, and ran.

You don't want to know what happened next. Let's just say I wasn't fast enough, OK?

The other dream featured me on a pitcher's mound, but the mound was in an operating room. I was trying to take some warm-up pitches, but there were a couple of things hindering me. One: I was wearing nothing but a hospital gown and my cleats. Two: There were people all around me, staring. My real-life orthopedic surgeon was there, holding a scalpel. So was my baseball coach, but he was carrying a chain saw. Then there was a whole ring of other spectators that kept shifting in and out of focus like reality does in dreams. I would catch glimpses of my mom, my dad, my older sister, Samantha (who's been away at college for a year already), random kids from school. The ice cream man from my block. A scary clown.

Coach and the surgeon were jostling each other for position next to me, arguing like little kids: "Me first!" "No, me!" "Tell you what. How 'bout if it's a fastball, I get him, and if it's a curveball, you get him?"

"No, he's mine! Finders, keepers!"

I looked in at my catcher. Of course, it was AJ — but a mean-looking, evil AJ. He flashed me the sign: his thumb and forefinger joined together to form a zero. I shouted out, "Is that a one or a two?" He just threw down the same sign again, emphatically. Then I felt a searing pain in my throwing arm, and woke up screaming.

After a few nights of this, I was sitting in my kitchen at two A.M. with my mom. Ever since I was little, she has always heard me whenever I've woken up in the night. We have this tradition: I pour us both some milk, she grabs some vanilla wafer cookies, and then I tell her my problems while we eat our snack. Meanwhile, my father and Samantha have always just slept right through everything.

I secretly love those times. They're comforting. I mean, the milk is cold, the cookies are good, and Mom is usually a great listener. Unless, that is, you're trying to talk to her about a strange blanking-out episode her father had. Then she just shuts down.

"You don't understand, Mom," I said. "He totally froze. You know how he always says, *Gotta get the shot?* That's, like, his life's motto. But he just sat there and let the eagle fly by."

"Honey, your grandfather has been shooting pictures for a long time. He knows what he's doing. Maybe he just thought the light was bad, or the angle was wrong, or something."

"Mom, he told me he'd been going there for thirty years, waiting for an eagle to fly by early in the morning. Then one does, and he doesn't take a single shot? There's something wrong. I'm telling you."

"Peter, people's reflexes slow down when they get older. And your grandfather is seventy-eight years old. He probably just couldn't react fast enough."

"No, I saw his face after. It was like he wasn't there, Mom. He just completely spaced out for, I don't know, at least a minute. And then he was confused for a while, like he wasn't sure what we were doing on top of the mountain."

"I don't know. He seemed fine when you got home."

"He didn't seem fine. *He gave me his cameras!* To keep! He told me they were mine now. That's not fine."

For a moment, Mom looked shaken by this piece of info. But then she said, "Oh, Peter. He was probably just trying to give you something to do with your time — you've been so mopey lately, ever since the . . . uh . . . Anyway, maybe he thought you could get some good use out of the equipment."

"Yeah, he gave me the whole speech about finding a hobby or whatever. But I'm telling you, Mom: This was bigger than that."

"Well, we can keep an eye on him, honey. All right?"

I nodded, and went back to my room. But I knew she still couldn't understand. She hadn't seen what I had seen.

Mom didn't know this, but my nighttime ritual wasn't over at that point. Ever since my last baseball game, when I went back upstairs, I would turn on my computer and spend another hour or so flipping back and forth between a folder on my hard drive and a set of favorites on the Internet. It's sad, really: All across America, untold thousands of teenagers were downloading music illegally, bullying other kids online, searching for sexy pictures, finding bomb-making recipes, hacking the Pentagon's computers. Me, I always did the same exact thing every time. I would click into the "My Photos" folder and look through hundreds and hundreds of sports pictures my grandfather had taken of me since I was a little kid playing T-ball. The doctors had told me I would never pitch again, so I didn't know why I was torturing myself, but there I was. Click! I'm six years old, running for first base with all my might. Click! I'm seven, looking very serious at the plate, facing a real live kid pitcher for the first time. Click! I'm eight, accepting the Player of the Year award. Click! I'm nine, ten, eleven, leaning forward on the mound, cool and composed, ready to mow down batter after batter.

Sitting cross-legged on my bed with my laptop, I can feel the seams of an imaginary baseball against my fingertips. Sometimes, I even catch myself switching grips over and over again: four-seam fast-ball, two-seam fastball, cutter, change.

When this has gone far beyond unbearable, I go to the favorites folder. "Favorites" is a pretty ironic word for what's in there. What I have is a set of maybe a dozen web pages about an injury called osteochondritis dissecans: my injury. I know you probably haven't heard of it. I hadn't, either, until the doctors broke the news to me after several X-rays and an MRI. Basically, I should have told my parents about the stupid pain in my elbow. And because I hadn't, because I had kept pitching when I should have stopped, I had worn out my elbow joint. The cartilage at the end of my upper arm bone had lost its blood supply, died, and cracked off. Then the sur-geon had had to go in there, fish out the broken-off pieces that were jamming up the joint, carve away some more unhealthy cartilage, reshape the end of the bone, close me up, and hope for the best.

"The best," as in, "You'll never pitch again, but maybe you won't have crippling arthritis in your arm before you're thirty."

By the second week of school, I had such big bags under my eyes, I looked like a bad-guy alien from *Star Wars*. Or a rabid raccoon. Of course, our first assignment in photography class was to do a portrait of a partner. And naturally, I got assigned to the only other freshman in the class: Angelika Stone. Tidbits Girl.

The school cameras had been fancy when they were new but were kind of primitive now, and we couldn't use studio lighting or camera flashes because everyone was shooting in the same room. I knew my grandfather's amazing lenses would work better in low light than anything the class had, but I would have felt a little weird bringing in his $1,500 Nikon with its $500 portrait lens. Anyway, I figured Angelika was so pretty, I'd get a good grade no matter what I did.

When shooting time came, Angelika wanted me to pose first. I felt like the biggest idiot in the world sitting there with my shadowed eyes, in a grungy long-sleeved Philadelphia 76ers jersey, my hair spiking in random directions.

I gave it a good effort, though. Angelika made posing fun by pretending this was a real modeling shoot.

In fact, she was so loud about it that I thought the upperclassmen were going to smack her, or officially shun us, or something: "Work those lips, Petey! Really give it to me! Love the camera! *Lo-o-ove* the camera!" So I worked the lips. I really gave it to her. I lo-o-oved the camera. We were having a great time until Mr. Marsh came over, looked at Angelika's photos in the camera's viewfinder, and started critiquing:

"Angelika, what do ya see in your mind when ya pic-chuh Pee-tuh? Ya need to know what ya want before ya shoot. I mean, you guys can edit the shots all you want aftah — you can work togethah on the editing, by the way — but it's always bettah if yer raw material has a *direction*. Is Pee-tuh a serious person? Are ya goin' for gravity — the Abe Lincoln effect? Is he gorgeous — are ya going in a *GQ* direction? Is he mysterious? Ya need to develop a *concept*! Think about what ya want the *world* to see through your lens!"

OK, it was cheesy, embarrassing, fortune-cookie-wisdom stuff, but I could handle it. Until Mr. Marsh started getting technical:

"And then there are the, um, cosmetic issues. That hair" — actually, he said "hay-uh" — "are ya going Wild Man of Borneo on purpose? The skin — are ya gonna get rid of that shine in Photoshop afterward? We might have a filter that would help. It's always easier to fix the image than to deal with the blemishes in processing. Oooh, and the glare from his glasses. Again, ya could go with a filtuh now, or . . ."

I have to admit, I sort of tuned out the rest of the speech. In fact, I asked to be excused and headed for the rest room. By the time I got back, Mr. Marsh had moved on to his next victim, and I thought the worst was over.

That's what I get for being optimistic. The instant my butt hit the chair, Angelika went to work on me. She produced a hairbrush and made me do a reasonable facsimile of self-grooming. Then she made me take my glasses off. I hate having my glasses off in public. First of all, when you've been wearing glasses since the second grade, everyone tells you how weird you look when you take them off, and second of all, I feel vulnerable when I can't freaking *see*. But I didn't want to mess up Angelika's grade or anything.

"So," I said, trying to make some small talk, "what's your *concept* for me? Are we going with Rugged, Yet Vulnerable? Mister Smooth Goes to High School? The Handsome Stranger?"

I think she smiled, although I couldn't actually see her expression without my glasses. "Actually, I'm thinking Dork Boy Gets a Makeover. What do you think? Genius, right?"

I gritted my teeth and growled, "Just remember, soon *I'll* be the one with the camera."

Angelika snapped off a few frames, then decided to move me closer to the windows in order to get some more natural light. Sure enough, with the tiny apertures of the school's lenses, it was pretty hard to get a well-exposed photo without using a flash. It was kind of warm near the window, so I pushed up the sleeves of my jersey. Then Angelika asked me to lean forward on my forearms against a stool. I did, and she said, "Better . . . better . . . that light gives your skin a nice glow . . ."

A nice glow? Was that a good thing for skin to have? Why was glow good if shine was bad? Whatever, if she was happy, I could roll with it. I flexed my forearms. Angelika gasped. *Hey,* I thought, *I know I'm built, but this is a little bit much, don't you think?*

Then I realized what Angelika must have seen: my surgery scars. They're pretty hideous, so I understood the reaction. I yanked down my sleeves in a hurry. I tried really hard to read Angelika's expression, but everything was too blurry, so I grabbed my glasses and shoved them on. I caught Angelika's eyes darting away from their focus on my arm, just as she said, "What?"

"What do you mean, what? You saw my scars."

"Uh, those little things around your elbow? They're hardly noticeable. Really. You just, um, surprised me. That's all. No big deal. Come on, let's finish shooting before we run out of time, OK?"

This was weird. She had definitely been staring, but now she wasn't going to be nosy about it? I felt my face flushing, a look I did not need to have immortalized on film, so I said, "Why don't we take a break and see what we've got so far?" She agreed, and we took the memory card out of our camera and hooked it up to the card reader at the closest computer workstation.

You know what? Looking at hugely magnified close-ups of myself with an attractive girl whom I barely even knew was even less relaxing than it sounds. Also, the pictures were technically awful. The ones from before we'd moved to the window had probably looked OK on the tiny viewing screen of the camera, but on the monitor they were way underexposed, which meant that there were massive, gloomy shadows everywhere. The areas under my eyes looked caked in black makeup, like I was trying out to be the bass player in an emo band. Plus, I didn't look posed enough, somehow. In every frame there was some problem with timing: I wasn't quite looking at the camera, or my mouth was dangling open, or I was slouched over.

"Yuck," Angelika said.

"Thanks," I replied.

"No, not you," she said. "It's the camera. It has a really horrible shutter lag, so every time I tried to get a good shot, by the time the autofocus locked in, it was too late. And the exposure . . . that's all my fault."

I reached for the mouse, then clicked down through the photos on screen until we got to the ones we'd taken by the window. "Maybe you had better luck with the brighter light," I said. But if anything, the brighter shots were worse. They were so overexposed I looked like a ghost. Or a perfectly white mannequin with a deep-black wig. I kept clicking until the last few frames were up. I looked really closely at those, partly because I wanted to see how horrible my elbow looked, and partly because I wanted to see whether Angelika had focused in on it. But the shots were so washed-out you couldn't really even tell that my arm was an arm.

Angelika sighed, said, "I give up," clicked out of the screen, and ejected the memory card. Then she flipped the card into my hands, slung the camera into my lap, and said, "Your turn, Pete. Make me a star!"

I know this isn't going to make sense to anyone who isn't a camera nerd like I am, but I couldn't even stand the thought of using such inferior equipment for anything I was being graded on. After my grand-father's stuff, this was like asking a fighter pilot to fly a hot-air balloon. As Angelika tried sitting at differ-ent angles on the stool by the window, I tried to find some decent menu options for programming the camera, but there were huge gaps between the available shutter speeds, the maximum aperture of the lens was pathetic, and the ISOs only went up to 800, instead of the 25,600 on Grampa's Nikons. Put into simple English, what this meant was that there was no way I could get any kind of decent shot.

That's why I said what I said next. Even if it came out sounding totally wrong, I was just trying to put some effort into the first graded project of my high school career. "Listen, Angelika, why don't we meet up at my house to work on this? I, um, I have much nicer equipment."

Oh, God, I thought as soon as it was too late. *That sounded wildly inappropriate.* Angelika pushed her glasses down her nose a bit, peered over them at me, and said, "Ooh, I'd love to come to your house and check out your equipment." Then she laughed and added, "But don't you think you're moving a little fast?"

Why is it that every single desirable female I've ever met can make me feel like an idiot in five seconds flat?

5. talking
man-to-man

A few days later, AJ invited himself over to my house to shoot baskets. He only lives a couple of blocks away, and he used to have to walk right past my door to get to middle school, so we've probably spent five hundred hours playing basketball in my driveway. Now, you're probably thinking, "How can you shoot baskets if you're not medically cleared to play sports?" The answer is that I can't. Which leads to the next logical question: "What kind of insensitive weenie would invite himself over to his best friend's house to do something his friend would totally kill to do, but isn't allowed to?"

I find myself having those kinds of thoughts all the time, but that's just AJ. I love the guy, but he barely seems to notice that other human beings have emotions, so he says and does completely offensive stuff at random moments without a shred of explanation. Once, in seventh grade, I had a huge argument with AJ because he wouldn't stop saying my sister was "suh-mokin' hottt!" I ended up storming out of his house. When I got home, I was so mad that I told Samantha what had happened, and she said, "Ooh, that's so cute! You have to understand, Petey, your friend AJ is essentially a caveman. He only has three feelings: hungry, hyper, and horny. He's a great kid if you can just resign yourself to that. And maybe throw him some chunks of raw meat or something once in a while to keep him happy."

My sister is a genius judge of character.

So there I was, sitting on my butt, cooking in the Indian summer sun and watching my caveman buddy take about forty-three million foul shots. As an added bonus, he was enlightening me with his insights about the female mind. "So then" — grunt, shoot, swish — "she just invited herself over here and told you to take pictures of her?"

"No," I said, "that's not what happened at all. Mr. Marsh assigned us to be partners, and then —"

"She wants you, man."

"What are you talking about? I just said the teacher *assigned* us to work together. And then I was the one who asked *her* to come over."

"Oh, yeah" — grunt, shoot, swish — "she totally wants you."

I stood up, walked over to AJ, and knocked on the side of his head. "Are you listening to me at all? The teacher made the assignment, and then I made the invitation."

He pushed me away with one hand, and shot with the other. It was a complete air ball, and he said, "See, now you made me miss. Like it's *my* fault you can't accept what's happening in your love life."

I sat back down in disgust. "My *love life?*"

He smirked. "Yup. See, she made you invite her over here. First she arranged to be in your class. Then she probably knew you'd be the only two freshmen in there, so she would be your partner. Her final sly move was to use her femi-mind tricks to control you into asking her out."

"Femi-mind tricks?"

"Yeah. All the high school girls have 'em."

I stared at AJ blankly. He's used to that, so when he's on a roll, it doesn't affect him. He continued as though I were leaning forward on one arm, looking up at him in an awed silence. "See, you know how there's, like, band camp and football camp and stuff right before school starts?"

I nodded as slightly as possible. I didn't want to indicate any sort of agreement or anything.

"Well, for girls, I've heard there's this special kind of camp that we're not supposed to even know about. For maybe three days before freshman year, they go up to the high school for, like, hormone boot camp. I'm pretty sure the instructors are the senior cheerleaders or something. Anyway, the girls master essential feminine wiles, and then they use 'em on us."

"Um, and you know this how?"

"Because of Elena Zubritskaya."

Elena Zubritskaya was this girl who had moved to our town from Russia in seventh grade. She was short and petite, with dark hair and glasses. In middle school, she had been quiet, shy, and mostly invisible. I hadn't seen her around in high school so far, but I guess AJ had.

"What about her?"

"What about her? What *about* her? Have you been walking the hallways *blindfolded* for the past two weeks? She went away for the summer a mouse, and came back a raging tigress!"

"Really? Little Elena?"

"Believe me, Pete, you are the last male in the world who's still thinking of her as 'little' Elena. She's a whole new woman. I mean, she always had a raging body . . ."

(She did? I honestly, honestly had never noticed.)

". . . but now she's *working* it. I mean, the girl is *strutting* through the building. She has completely morphed into a bespectacled love goddess! Plus, you know how she didn't used to talk a whole lot, and we thought she couldn't even speak English? Now she's like 'So heavy this books,' and eleven guys suddenly appear to help her with her bag. Or she'll go 'I no have pencil,' and instantly, there's seventeen guys standing around her with pencils in their hands. She might not have her grammar down yet, but she's suddenly fluent in the international language of love. And she's leaving a trail of destruction. It's sick."

AJ took a break from talking to practice driving toward the hoop, while I sat there trying to follow what Elena Zubritskaya had to do with Angelika, or with AJ's imaginary secret hot-girl boot camp. AJ isn't a big fan of silence, though, so eventually he started lecturing me again. "So you see, Pete, that's how I know this Angelika babe is bent on dominating and controlling your mind."

"And what do you think I'm supposed to do about this?"

He tried a behind-the-back layup, watched the ball rattle around the rim before rolling off, and said, "Any control you think you have is an illusion. I recommend you just let it happen."

I pondered this for a while. Then I picked out what I thought was one of the bigger gaping flaws in his so-called logic. "OK, then. Let's just say Elena has suddenly been endowed with some kind of Victoria's Secret mojo."

"Oh, she has. She totally has."

"Whatever. She's not using it on any one specific guy, right? She's just captivating every guy in sight."

"So?"

"So, even if I think Angelika might be flirting with me specifically, she's probably not. She's probably just using her femi-mind tricks on everyone, and I happen to be sitting next to her in one of her classes." I couldn't help but notice that, despite the blatant insanity of this whole discussion, AJ now had me using his daffy new word. I swear, he's insidious.

"Well, then, either she is flirting with you deliberately, or she's flirting with you deliberately. Which means she is, in fact, flirting with you deliberately."

"Wha-a-at?"

"See, if she weren't, you wouldn't wonder if she was. But you *are* wondering, which means she is."

I pinched the bridge of my nose right above my glasses. My head was starting to hurt. "Even assuming that she is interested in me, why in the world would she be? We just met. I don't know anything about her, and she doesn't know anything about me. We've barely even talked."

"That's perfect. You're a mysterious stranger on a train."

"Huh?"

"Women like mysterious guys. Trust me: It's well-known."

"Well, what happens when I stop being a stranger on a train? I mean, after all this flirting, won't she eventually get to know me?"

"Yeah, so?"

"Won't that be the end of the mystery?"

"Sure, but then she'll like you for all of your studly attributes."

"Like what? My commanding five feet of height? My keen eyesight?"

"No, you're an athlete. Women love athletes."

Again with the insensitiveness. Insensitivity? Whatever, here was AJ, blundering in and stomping on my biggest sore spot. "Uh, in case you haven't noticed, I'm not an athlete anymore."

"Yes, you are. You're an injured athlete. They love that, too. You're like a wounded bird she can nurse back to health."

"But what if I'm never nursed back to health? The doctor said I might not pitch again." Actually, I was being dishonest. The doctor had flat-out said that I WOULD never pitch again.

"Meh, he was wrong."

I glared. AJ ignored. "I'm serious, Pete. And even if he was right, you just won't pitch. You can be our catcher."

"*Our* catcher?"

"You know, on the JV team."

"First of all, I can't play catcher, either. What if someone is stealing second base? How am I supposed to throw the ball down? What am I going to do, send it there by FedEx?"

"OK, you can play first, then. Lots of lefties play first. Plus, none of this will matter, because you're going to be fine. If doctors knew everything, they wouldn't get sued for malpractice, would they?"

AJ didn't get it. I would still have to throw the ball

65

sometimes, even to play first. And I was never going to be allowed to throw again. But *of course* he didn't get it, because I never came right out and told him. I had never come out and told him the whole truth about my diagnosis, my surgery, the physical therapy — anything. Maybe it was just because I hated thinking about the details. Maybe it was because I didn't want him to think I was a wuss. And maybe in a small, little part of the back of my mind, I was afraid he wouldn't hang out with me anymore if I was a lost cause.

"My prediction, Petey, is that by springtime, you'll be totally good to go."

I gave up on the baseball argument and changed the subject. Just talking about throwing a ball made me feel all panicky, anyway. "But then I won't be a wounded stranger bird on a train anymore. So won't Angelika lose interest?"

"Nah, by then you'll be, like, soul mates."

Not for the first time, I wished I could be AJ. It wasn't only that he had a healthy throwing arm — it was that he always believed good things would happen. Reality didn't even enter the picture. "All righty," he said, "I'll make you a deal. If I hit my next three free throws, Angelika and you are meant to be."

"Oh, because you control my destiny with your ability to make your foul shots?"

He nodded, and started dribbling the ball.

"But you don't control my mind, right? Angelika controls that?"

He nodded again, shot, and scored. Twice.

"And what about my free will?"

Dribble, shoot, swish. "Dude. Who needs free will when you've got Angelika?"

My grandfather came over for dinner that night. Mom wasn't saying much, Dad was still at work, and Grampa was as quiet as usual. I hadn't seen him since the day he had given me his cameras, and I was totally on edge. I was scrutinizing his every move, looking for signs that he was going senile. Mom would say, "Pass the peas, Dad," and I'd be like *Does he remember what peas are? Whew, he does. But did he pause for a minute to think, or did he recognize the peas right away? OK, I'll give him a 10 for "identifies vegetables."*

Dinner gets kind of long when you're concentrating that hard on something so horrible. When everyone was done, Mom volunteered to do the dishes so "You boys can enjoy some male bonding." Male bonding? What were we going to do, drink three beers and then shoot a moose?

Thinking of the word "shoot" reminded me of the forthcoming portrait date with Angelika. I told Grampa about it, and he asked, "Have you ever shot a serious portrait before?"

"No, but I've helped you do it a bunch of times. I've been with you at the studio for hundreds of engagement photos and stuff — I know what camera settings to use and everything."

He said, "Are you sure? It's different when you're the one in charge of the shoot. Plus, sometimes with a live model, you forget what you're doing. The pressure and all . . ."

"I know what I'm doing."

"Well, you want to be absolutely positive. Especially with an attractive young lady sitting in front of you, you might find it hard to concentrate."

"How do you know she's attractive?"

He raised an eyebrow. "You just told me."

See, he's totally fine, I told myself. *His wit is as sharp as ever, and he can still read me like my thoughts are engraved on my forehead. But wait, if he's in such great shape, why did he give me all of his cameras and everything?* I almost asked him about the cameras right then and there, but then I got an idea. I thought, *What if I do some photography stuff with him? Maybe something might come up. . . .*

"Grampa," I said, "I *might* need some practice before Angelika comes over. Do you think maybe you could sit for me?"

"Me?" he said. "I don't know what kind of practice that will be. I hope to God this girl doesn't look remotely like your old, shriveled grandfather."

"Oh, come on. I just need somebody to sit there and let me get all the equipment set up and ready.

That way I won't have to, um, fiddle around when Angelika is here."

Grampa's eyebrow shot up again, but thankfully, he didn't comment. And he followed me into the basement, where all the photography stuff was. Then he got right down to business. As I set out a stool for him, he fired off a series of questions:

"Are you going to shoot straight on or in profile?"

"With flash or without?"

"Lights and reflectors, or no?"

"Head and shoulders, or full-length?"

"Color or black-and-white?"

"What lens are you going to use? Do you want a blurred background, or do you want sharp focus all the way to the backdrop? Are you going to shoot automatic or manual? Have you charged an extra battery? Always charge an extra battery. And have some drinks ready, especially if you plan to have her under the lights for a while. It gets hot under the lights."

For a little while, as I scrambled to work out everything I had to do for this shoot, I told myself I had been crazy. Grampa was fine. He had thought of a million laser-sharp questions on the spot — and I had probably only considered half of them ahead of time. He actually *was* saving me from looking like a moron in front of Angelika.

When I was ready, Grampa sat very solemnly and looked at me with great gravity. I checked the light meter on the camera, moved one of the lights a little closer to his stool, and started snapping away. I took maybe twenty pictures from the front, and another fifteen from the sides, moving closer and farther from him. I just couldn't seem to get a decent shot, though. Grampa noticed my frustration, I guess, because he said, "If the setup isn't working, don't keep banging your head against the wall. Try something different."

"Like what?" I asked.

"How should I know?" he replied. "You're the photographer."

Then I had an idea: I turned off all of the lights on

one side of Grampa, and switched the camera from color to black-and-white. With one peek through the viewfinder, I knew I had it right now: every line in Grampa's face, every shadow around his eyebrows, stood out in stark relief. Before, he had just been some old guy in a chair. Now the image I was seeing had real, magnetic power.

I snapped off three shots from slightly different angles, but as soon as I peeked back at the first one, I knew I had my shot. I couldn't wait to get this loaded onto my computer and show him how great it had come out. I knew he was always an incredible stickler about cleaning up and packing everything away after a shoot, so I put everything away very neatly. I covered every lens, double-checked that I had turned off the camera, zipped everything into the camera bag, and then double-checked all the zippers and buckles on the bag. Grampa once told me he'd forgotten to check his bag's straps on a shoot at the Grand Canyon, and watched in horror as two of his favorite lenses had gone bouncing and smashing off the edge and into the gorge hundreds of feet below. I wanted him to know I had been listening.

I got everything squared away and turned back to Grampa. He was leaning forward on the stool, looking expectant. "Hey," he said, "I don't have all day. Are you going to take my picture, or what?"

6. peter friedman, ace newshound

If you don't want to have lots of unexpected hassles in your life, my advice is that you should never be too good at anything. I mean, if Angelika and I hadn't done such great work on our portraits, the rest of my year would have been about ten million times easier.

She came over on a Saturday afternoon. I had no idea what to expect. Was this a date? Because aside from meeting up with a bunch of girls at the ice skating rink every Saturday in middle school, and that one time I fooled around with Sheldon Kleiderman's cousin Abigail in an empty Hebrew school classroom during Sheldon's bar mitzvah, I wasn't exactly the king of experience in the chicks-'n'-babes department.

And did I want it to be a date? I mean, Angelika was so cute it made me uncomfortable to look at her, but then again, if I fell for every girl who made me uncomfortable, I'd never get anything done. Plus, aside from being cute, who knew what she was like? I knew nothing about this girl. Maybe she was a cute, boring nerd. A cute, vicious psycho. A cute axe murderer.

Just in case, I spent the whole morning running around cleaning everything. I even vacuumed the basement while my mother stared in shock. Then there was the frantic and repeated use of mouth-wash, the agonized checking and rechecking of wardrobe, even the ultra-long shower, which lasted until the water started losing heat and my father yelled through the door, "What are you doing in there, Pete? Your *sister* never took a shower this long!"

For the record, I am not so sure that was true.

But eventually, cleaned, jeaned, and fresh of breath, I stood at the doorway and let Angelika into my would-be love lair. Admittedly, both of my parents were hovering around and gawking, which wouldn't have been my choice for setting up a steamy photo-shoot atmosphere. And when the awkward introductions were done and Angelika and I went down to the basement, my mom made a big show of leaving the cellar door wide-open behind us.

I figured at least I was a nice-smelling child of embarrassing stalkers.

As soon as we were alone — or at least semi-alone — Angelika said, "So where's all this fancy equipment I've been hearing about?"

Why did everything this girl said have to sound so flirtatious, like each sentence had some hidden meaning? I decided she was probably talking about Grampa's cameras and lenses. Probably. I opened up the camera backpack and took out Grampa's main camera body, along with two different portrait lenses. "Um, well, h-here's what I thought I'd use to start with," I stammered. "I think it makes sense to try for some, uh, full-body shots" — UGH, that sounded sleazy — "and then, if we don't like what we're getting, we can get a little closer in. With this telephoto lens, I mean. Not like I'd be, uh, getting closer to you. Uh."

That's great, I thought. *End a freaking sentence with "Uh," why don't you? Smooth.*

She giggled, then got serious. "Sounds like a plan." She pointed to the stool I had set up for my grandfather during his practice shoot. "Is this where you want me?"

That was when the sweat started to soak through under my arms. "Yeah," I said, grabbing the camera and rotating the first lens into place. I looked through the eyepiece at her, at which point I realized she was wearing a white shirt, and I had hung a white backdrop. If I took the pictures this way, Angelika would look like the world's cutest floating head. I got to work switching backgrounds, while Angelika asked me personal questions. I've always hated personal questions, but at least it was better than sweating into the awkward silence.

"So where'd you get all this gear?" she said.

"Uh, my grampa. My grandfather. Paul Goldberg. He was a professional photographer. Maybe you've heard of Goldberg Photo? He did weddings, parties, commercial shoots. . . . He even won a lifetime achievement award from *Modern Bride* magazine."

"Doesn't he have a truck with a yellow mountain on it?"

I nod.

"I think I've seen it around town. So, uh, he left you this stuff in his will? That's really touching."

"No, he's not dead or anything. He's retired, that's all. Over the summer, he decided he'd had enough of photography and gave everything to me. I mean, we always did a lot of shooting together anyway, plus he's getting older and he just —"

"Can't shoot anymore, huh?"

I turned and looked at her. Of course, I'd had that very same thought, but I didn't like hearing somebody else say it. "He *could* still shoot. He just decided it was time to quit."

"Suddenly?"

"Yeah, why?"

"Um, please don't take this the wrong way, but what you're saying about your grandfather reminds me of something that happened with my grandmother. She used to love playing bridge with her friends every Tuesday and Thursday, and then one day she stopped going. Dad asked her about it, and she said, 'What the hell is the point of playing if I can't keep track of the cards?' We had noticed she was starting to forget things, but we didn't know it was such a big deal. Until all of a sudden, it was. Has your grandfather been . . . well . . . different lately?"

I thought I knew what she meant, but that didn't mean I wanted to admit it. "Different how?"

"Well, for one thing, before he gave you his stuff, did you notice him making any unusual mistakes?"

I thought about that eagle flying right across Grampa's viewfinder, and nodded.

"Spacing out? Maybe forgetting common words once in a while?"

Again, I saw the eagle. Then I remembered something else: Once, in July, we had been sitting at a diner having breakfast. He had been sugaring up his coffee, and then when he was ready for the creamer, he said, "Pete, please pass me the . . . uh . . . white stuff." Was that a danger sign?

I nodded.

"And then, out of the blue, he quit photography?"

"Yeah."

She nodded slowly. "Just got disgusted and walked away, right?"

"Yes, but — what are you trying to say?"

"Peter, my grandmother had Alzheimer's disease."

I had heard the term but wasn't one hundred percent sure what it meant.

"That's when an older person's brain deteriorates faster than normal."

Aha. "Wait, I didn't say his brain was abnormal or anything, I just said —"

Angelika cut me off. "Does he seem OK most of the time?"

It was my turn to nod.

"But then all of a sudden, he blanks out?"

"Yeah, but my mom said he's fine. And he's her dad — she knows him better than I do."

"My grandma was my dad's mother. He insisted

that she was fine, too. And then one day we went over there for Sunday dinner and found her standing at the head of the table, trying to carve a raw chicken."

Swell.

"But the first signs were when she started dropping out of activities, like the incident with the cards. Sound familiar?"

Grampa had never played bridge, but other than that, yeah. I didn't feel like hearing any more about this, so I said, "I don't know. Can we try shooting now?"

Unlike AJ, I guess Angelika could tell when to let a subject drop, because she smiled brightly, struck a pose on the stool, and said, "I'm ready for my close-up now!" I was really, really glad I had practiced this with Grampa and gotten all the camera settings right, because he had been telling the truth: It was hot under the lights, and looking at Angelika made it terribly hard for me to think clearly. The whole situation just seemed so — I don't know — *Sports Illustrated* swimsuit edition–esque.

Don't get me wrong. Angelika obviously wasn't wearing a bikini or anything, just jeans and a white dress shirt with a collar. But she was smiling and pouting, crossing and uncrossing her legs, and sticking her tongue out of the corner of her mouth once in a while. And me? I was dying.

When we took a break to switch lenses, I got her a glass of water. She gulped it down in about three seconds, which made me wonder if she was thinking, um, impure thoughts, too, or just having a field day putting them in my head. I just kept telling myself, *Chill, chill, chill. You don't know this girl. You don't know this girl. You don't know this girl. Sure, she's funny. And smart. And hot. And OH, HOLY COW, DID SHE JUST FIX HER BRA STRAP? Wait, what was I saying again?*

Eventually, when the basement was starting to feel like Satan's private sauna, my mother came downstairs to offer us homemade brownies. Angelika turned to see what my mom was carrying, and without thinking, I snapped off three frames of her face just as she set her eyes on the brownies and smiled.

This wasn't like the sexy, posed smiles Angelika had been working for the past half hour, or the smirk she put on in class while she was making sarcastic anti-teacher comments. It was just real. She looked almost like a little kid for a second or two.

When Mom had gone back upstairs, we fired up my computer and looked over everything we had gotten. And you know what? Those three shots of Angelika looking at the brownies were *the* ones. Which proves two things:

- Like Grampa always told me, you can't force the shot . . .
- . . . but when the perfect image presents itself, you've got to be ready.

Next we shot maybe fifty pictures of me, and then my dad came downstairs to tell us Angelika's mother was at the door. Angelika took the memory card with her, so I had no idea whether she had gotten any good shots, but that was OK. I knew I had aced my half of the assignment. Plus, wow. I was almost starting to think AJ had been right: Angelika was giving off signals — signals so strong even a moron like me could pick up on them.

Now all I had to do was figure out what to do next. And, barring a sudden and unforeseen bar mitzvah party, I had no clue how this part was supposed to happen.

At our next photography class, Angelika came in with a huge smile on her face and her hands behind her back. I could tell she was holding something but couldn't tell what it was. I asked her what she was hiding, but she just ignored me and edged her way over to her seat. I asked again, and she said, "You'll see."

I asked, "Can I see it now?" and Angelika shook her head. I said, "Pretty please?" and she shook her head again. Then she winked. So I tried to reach around her back with one hand, but she twisted away. I reached around with the other hand, too, which meant I had my arms completely around Angelika when Mr. Marsh walked in. I could feel two things: First, she was holding one of those cardboard tubes you put posters in, and second, I really didn't want to let go.

Until Mr. Marsh cleared his throat behind me. Angelika and I separated in a big hurry, while the upperclassmen all around us laughed. As we scrambled into our seats, I distinctly heard Erika, one of the senior girls, say, "Ooh, look, the fur-resh-mannnnnn is turning red. It's just so adorable!" I don't know why all these older women think the word "freshman" has three syllables.

Anyway, Mr. Marsh said, "I hate to interrupt yer . . . ahem . . . social time, but we gotta get started. Now, what's that yer holdin', Miss Stone?"

Angelika didn't look half as mortified as I did. In fact, she seemed kind of pleased with herself. "It's our project, Mr. Marsh. We did our portraits at Peter's house on Saturday, and then I went home and worked on the images in Photoshop. Peter hasn't seen them yet, so I was, um, hiding the tube when you walked in."

The only senior guy in the class, Danny something, whispered so everybody could hear,

"Ooh, they're playing Hide the Tube! Way to go, little fur-resh-mannnnnn!"

Apparently, senior guys say it that way, too. *Kill me*, I thought.

"May I see the photos?" Mr. Marsh asked, ignoring the tide of laughter that was breaking across the classroom. He made a beckoning gesture, so Angelika stood and brought him the tube. Then, right in front of everyone, he took the cap off of one end, and pulled out a bunch of rolled 11 x 14 inch prints. One by one, he hung the prints from clips over the whiteboard. Next, he asked the whole class to gather around and see.

I kind of wished I were still across the hall in the boring beginners' classroom with AJ. Because you know what? When you're bored, you're safe.

I was the last person to make my way to the board, which meant that I had to look over people to even see what the prints looked like. Danny and Erika parted to let me slide in, and I got my first look. Holy cow! The shots were amazingly good. Angelika had printed the best shot of herself smiling at the brownies three times, in three different ways. There was a sepia-toned one that looked like an antique, a black-and-white one that emphasized her dark hair and the gleam of her teeth, and finally, a highly processed color one that took my breath away. Angelika had edited the colors so that everything was washed out but her eyes and her lips.

Mr. Marsh gushed over our work, complimented me on the sharpness of the image, and then asked Angelika where she'd gotten so good at editing and printing. It turns out her mom is a graphic designer for a huge publishing company in Allentown, right near where we live. I couldn't believe Angelika hadn't mentioned that when I'd been bragging about my grandfather's photography career.

Note to self: Ask girls questions.

Angelika had printed three different shots of me. They weren't as amazing as the ones of her, which made sense because we had spent so much more time on shooting her, and of course because she was so much better-looking than me. They weren't terrible, but they weren't great, either. Mr. Marsh made some technical comments about the shots, and then said, "Well, kids, I am really impressed. For the prints of Angelika, ya both get an A. For the photos of Peetuh, I could give ya both a B now, or ya could go back and try ta shoot some more. Trootfully, I would encourage ya to take another stab at it. Ya seem ta enjoy each other's company, an' I wouldn't wanna leave ya wit' any . . . *unfinished business*. Heh-heh."

Heh-heh. It's really too bad students aren't allowed to throw cameras at their teachers.

As we headed back to our seats, Mr. Marsh dropped the bomb. "Ladies and gentlemen," he said, "as ya know, there is a lot of overlap between the yearbook and school newspaper staffs and the roster of this class. And as ya also know, many of yer assignments throughout this year will be used as material for the school publications."

Had we known those things? Everyone else seemed to be nodding in agreement, but as a furresh-mannnnnn who had basically been thrown into the class, I wasn't sure I had heard anything about joining the newspaper or the yearbook.

Mr. Marsh continued, "Anyway, this morning I received a very disturbing e-mail message from the school business office. Some of ya might remember that for the past several years, the school has outsourced all of our sports photography to Ackerman's Photo Studio here in town. Ya might also be aware of our district's budget crisis. Well, apparently, the school board has voted ta freeze the budget for this year and has also canceled all outstanding contracts."

One of the junior girls, Danielle, who was layout editor for the yearbook — which I knew because she mentioned it approximately every fifteen seconds — said, "So what are we going to do? We can't have a yearbook without sports pictures!"

Mr. Marsh said, "I have an idea, but it's gonna take a lot of extra work. I was thinking that maybe we could rearrange our class assignments so that you guys take the sports pictures. Does anybody here know anything about sports?"

The only sophomore boy in the class, James, said, "Well, I shot a sports spread for the newspaper last spring, remember?"

Danny leaned across his desk and stage-whispered, "Uh, Jimmy, I'm not sure chess really counts as a sport."

James turned and spat, "Oh, yeah, Mr. Big Shot Senior? And I suppose your status as cocaptain of the debate society makes you an expert on all things athletic?"

A junior named San Lee, who usually leaned way back in a chair in the corner of the back row and rarely spoke, sat up and said, "Guys, shooting sports is really tricky. We need somebody with a lot of experience, or the whole sports section of the yearbook is going to look like it was shot with a little kid's toy camera."

Angelika raised her hand. "Mr. Marsh, guess what? Pete and I are very experienced. I mean, at sports shooting . . ."

And that's how I became athletics coeditor of my high school yearbook.

7. wither or withouter

I haven't mentioned the worst thing about my arm situation yet, mostly because I hate thinking about it, and it's way worse than just not being able to throw. It's even worse than the scarring. The truth is, after my surgery, when all the splints, supports, and bandages came off, my left arm was super-weak, and the muscles were starting to get all shrunken and withered. I mean, I'm a sports guy. I've been working out every day of the week for years. Every time I've ever watched a ball game on TV, which was pretty much every night, I've done push-ups, sit-ups, and wrist curls on and off the whole time.

It's not like I was some huge hulk of muscle before my injury, but I was wiry. I was strong. So when the wrappings came off, and I saw how wimpy my forearm had become, I had to bite my lip to keep from crying. The doctors told me I'd be able to regain "much of the functionality" of the arm, which I'm sure they thought was very comforting. Then they sent me to physical therapy. All summer long, it was three afternoons a week. The first few weeks I wasn't even supposed to move my own stupid arm. The therapists would twist it and turn it, or put it in machines that rotated and revolved while I bit my lip until it bled.

I knew that stretching could hurt, but never like this. Just getting my arm extended until it was almost straight was like some horrible endurance event in the Cruelty Olympics. The hardest thing was that as soon as therapy was over for the day, the muscles would pull tight, and the arm would start to bend again.

How bad was it? There were nights when I could barely sleep from the cramping. And plenty of other nights when I did sleep, but the pain found its way into my every dream. During the day, I wore nothing but long sleeves from July through October just so nobody would have to look at my wimpy little jacked-up limb. I never told anybody how bad it all was, physically or mentally. The physical therapist would make me fill out these pain self-evaluation forms and I'd just check off whatever column was closest to fine.

There was no column for "epic arm fail" anyway.

After the weeks of "passive mobility" exercises — in case that wasn't too much of an oxymoron — the therapists made me start actually doing the stretching myself. Right around the time I became an official sports photographer, my arm was starting to feel a little looser. And then one day, when AJ had been bugging me again about getting back into pitching shape, I got home from school and the house was empty. So I went a little nuts.

I took my pitchback net out of the shed, grabbed a bucket of baseballs from the garage, and set myself up maybe twenty feet away from the target. I'm not stupid or anything, OK? I knew I had to be careful and take it slow. I wasn't trying to throw from a regulation distance right off the bat, and I definitely wasn't thinking I could throw anything resembling a real pitch.

Mostly, I just really missed standing there with a baseball in my hand.

I stood there for the longest time, with that sick-to-the-stomach feeling you get when you've broken your mother's favorite lamp or whatever, but she hasn't noticed yet. I could even feel my legs trembling a little. But I went ahead and cocked my left arm behind my head. Then I tossed the ball.

It went about three feet and plopped into the grass like a fat little dead pigeon. I sat down on the lawn and wept so hard I could barely breathe. Then I picked up the ball, dropped it into the bucket, carried the whole shebang over to our garbage can, and dumped it.

"A sports photographer, huh?" AJ asked me a few days later on the way home from school. "With Angelika? Suh-weet!"

"Yeah, but —"

"But what? She volunteered the two of you, right?"

"Yeah, but —"

"But nothing. You're gonna be hanging out together, like, nonstop."

"Yeah, but —"

"First you're going to go to all the games together, right?"

"Yeah, but —"

"And then you're going to have to edit the photos together. In the yearbook office. Wa-a-ay after school. Alone. It's gonna be, like, your office of lo-o-ove."

"Yeah, but —"

"Ooh, I know what you're going to say, though. What about baseball season, right? I mean you're good and all, but I don't see how even you can pitch and take pictures at the same time."

Yeah, I know I could have told him the whole truth then. Believe me, I know. But instead I just let him roll over me. As usual.

"But wait, that's perfect, Pete! Then she'll have to come take pics of you in action. And she'll be all, 'Wow, did you really just strike out thirteen batters in one game?' and 'Oh, Petey, your butt looks so *cute* in that uniform!'"

We stopped on the sidewalk in front of my house, and AJ said, "Uh, Pete, weren't you going to say something?"

"Nah, it's all good," I said. "I just, uh . . . oh, forget it."

"What, man? You can tell me anything. I trust you with all my secrets, don't I? I mean, that one time when we were in second grade and Nikki Krupnik kissed me in the coat closet, I told you. Am I right or am I right?"

I laughed. "Uh, AJ, you told me that because you *wanted* me to tell everybody. This is different."

AJ put on his most serious face and sat down on my front steps. And once again, I had the perfect opportunity to tell him. "Well, Pedro, what is it?"

I took a deep breath. Then I chickened out and came up with a weaselly half-truth. I mean, it was true, but it wasn't everything. "I don't know how to tell Angelika this. Or Mr. Marsh. But I'm supposed to take pictures of a volleyball game tonight. And . . ."

"And what?"

"And I don't know anything about shooting volleyball."

"What's there to know? You just point the camera wherever the ball is, and press the little button. Oh, and don't get all distracted by the bouncing babes in tight shorts."

"No, you don't understand. Shooting indoor gym sports is really complicated. The light is crappy, you can't use a flash because you'll blind the players, and the action happens really, really fast."

"And there are bouncing babes in tight shorts. Sorry, Petey, you just can't convince me that this is a problem. You'll figure it all out. Just don't stare too much, or Angie will get mad."

So there you have it, sports fans: The Official Caveman's Guide to Sports Photography.

That night, I found myself sitting on the top row of the bleachers next to Angelika, lined up with the volleyball net. I was weighed down with enough cameras, lenses, and other assorted gear to collapse the whole structure. Before heading out, I had called my grandfather for advice, and he had told me all I would need was one specific lens. But he had also once told me that it's better to carry three extra lenses, have a tired shoulder, and get your shot than to have a nice, light camera bag and miss the moment.

Angelika was going to be shooting, too. She was all set up with a pretty nice camera of her own. It was a Canon, which meant we couldn't share lenses, but it looked like she would do fine. The game started, and I learned something really fast: If you don't know the sport, you can be the freaking Michelangelo of photography, and you still won't get what you need. My camera was always pointed in the wrong direction; I missed every key play by a split second; I couldn't get the shutter speed fast enough to keep the pictures from getting blurred in the dim light. I felt completely overwhelmed. After one game, I was ready to quit. "What I really need," I said to Angelika, "is a pause button."

Angelika smiled, pointed to her camera's view-finder, and said, "No worries." Then she said, "Keep shooting, though, partner. Try to get at least one good shot of Number Nine spiking the ball, OK? She's the captain. I'll be down there for a while." Angelika pointed to an area right behind the back line of the court and a little bit off to one side. She took the long telephoto lens off of her camera and put on a much shorter one. Then she was off.

I watched her walk around the edge of the gym floor to her chosen spot, kneel down, and start shooting. *Wow,* I thought. *She called me "partner."* I got back to shooting, but as soon as I got a picture of the captain girl jumping and spiking, I switched subjects and took maybe forty shots of Angelika in profile. I don't know why exactly. I just did it.

After the match, in the middle of packing all our gear away, Angelika asked me for the memory card I had been using so she could go home and process the photos on it. Without thinking, I handed the card over. I called my parents on my cell phone for a ride, and it wasn't until I was halfway home that I realized Angelika would see all the footage of her.

Great, I thought. *There's nothing as thrilling for a girl as finding out her new coeditor is a stalker.*

• • • • • • • • • •

Freshman year rolled along, kind of. Well, parts of it rolled along, parts of it lurched along, and parts of it scraped and screeched along in the manner of scrap metal being dragged across a chalkboard. For me, class was easy. I aced all of my academic courses without too much sweat, and the extra time demands of my sudden editorial gig weren't anything compared to all the sports practices I'd always had before — between the lack of indoor baseball workouts and the fact that I wasn't playing basketball, I had more time than I knew what to do with. Home was a little weird, though. Mom still didn't want to hear there was anything wrong with her father. Dad was still working a million hours, and with Samantha off at college, the house was wa-a-ay too empty and quiet most of the time.

The scraping and screeching mostly came from inside my own head. I was still having nightmares about surgery, pitching, and my grampa all tumbled up together. Plus, I kept wanting to tell AJ I wasn't going to be his teammate ever again, but I was still chickening out. He was networking like a madman with a lot of the older athletes, especially once he made the JV basketball team, and he kept introducing me to everyone as "Peter Friedman, Future Star Pitcher." I wondered what he would call me if he learned the truth: "Peter Friedman . . . Uh, Some Kid with a Camera"? Or even worse, "Peter . . . Uh, Your Name *Is* Peter, Right?"

One Saturday, I went to Angelika's house so she could redo my portrait shots. Of course, I had tormented myself over what to wear, until I just gave up and threw on jeans and a New York Yankees T-shirt over a white long-sleeved Under Armour — which was basically my default outfit anyway. I met her mom, who had this smirk on her face the whole time, like *Oh, you're the boy that takes forty random pictures of my daughter, huh? Nice T-shirt, Stalker Boy!*

By the time I had smiled and bluffed my way through the maternal interview, I realized it had been a mistake to wear the Under Armour, because I was sweating bullets. AND I couldn't take it off, because then my jacked-up elbow would be on full photographic display.

Angelika had set up a little studio area in the dining room, with a gray backdrop pinned to the wall, and a wooden chair next to a row of north-facing windows. I sat in the chair, and even without any direct sunlight, I was cooking. Angelika sat on a stool about ten feet away, and picked up her camera. Then she put it down again, and said, "Hey, Pete, I've thought a lot about what was wrong with the shots we got last time, and I think I have it. You know how Mr. Marsh said I needed to come up with a concept?"

Angelika picked up a brown paper lunch bag that had been next to the stool, and looked away from me. Obviously, she was going to surprise me with something from the bag. I tried to work out what could be in there — Shades? Hair gel? A really, really tiny leather jacket? None of those things would be weird enough to make her break eye contact, though. As she so often did, Angelika had once again made me really curious and just a tad terrified at the same time.

"Uh, yeah," I said.

"Well, I think the problem is that I don't know what my concept is, because I don't know you."

"What do you mean? You've been to my house. We have class together every day. We're coeditors and everything."

She looked up from the bag, right into my eyes. "And you take lots of pictures of me when I'm not looking."

Whoa. I'd been wondering for weeks whether she was ever going to bring that up. Looked like this was my lucky day!

If you've noticed so far that I had been doing a lot of blushing and sweating in my ninth-grade year, you haven't seen anything compared to what was happening to me in that moment of Under Armoured bustedness. Plus, now I added stammering to my list of socially awkward panic symptoms. "Uh, I, um, I was just checking out the — the — the white balance setting on the camera. So I . . ."

Wow, Angelika's smirk looked remarkably like her mom's. "It's OK, Pete. I like it that you wanted to take pictures of me. I like *you*."

Good God.

"But," she continued, "I still don't know anything about you. And no offense, but you don't really, um, express your feelings much."

Sure I do, I thought. *I express my feelings by slowly drowning in my own undergarments.*

"So I went to your friend Adam."

Double good God. Adam is AJ's real name. I could only imagine what AJ might have told her about me.

"And I asked him for some ideas."

"Ideas about what?"

"Ideas for objects I could pose you with. Objects that are important to you."

Triple good God. What had he suggested: My old Rescue Heroes action figures? My childhood Buzz Lightyear night-light? A stack of dirty magazines? I was going to have to kill him.

She reached into the brown paper bag and pulled out something worse than all of those. I'll give you a hint: It was round and white, with curves of red stitching, and said OFFICIAL YOUTH TOURNAMENT APPROVED on the side. OK, so it would have been bad enough if AJ had just given her any old baseball, but he hadn't. This was an incredibly special baseball. It was the game ball from the best game AJ and I had ever had together.

"I can't believe you never told me what a super-star pitcher you are, Peter!" she said.

Were, I thought.

"Adam told me all about how you and he pitched a no-hitter together in the championship game two years ago. That must have been amazing! He even brought me a copy of the newspaper article. And he told me all about how you played hurt last year, and you were too brave to tell anybody."

Brave or moronic, I thought.

"He told me not to say anything about this, but he said you were training really hard to get back into playing condition for this spring, even though the doctors said you might not be able to play yet."

Kill me, I thought.

"So, umm, I had this idea that maybe I should take your picture holding the baseball. What do you think?"

I had no idea what to think.

"I mean, my mom said she thought it was a sexist idea for a photo shoot: Man with Tools. She said you didn't pose me with, like, a Betty Crocker baking set. But I wasn't trying to be like that. I just thought the baseball would show something deeper about who you are . . . that is, if you don't mind . . . Peter, would you please talk to me?"

I started to talk, but there was a catch in my throat. I cleared it, and tried again: "Gimme the ball."

"Really? You don't mind?"

I shook my head and held out my hand.

Angelika gave me the ball. I turned it over in my fingers, and a huge lump grew in my throat. Suddenly, in my own head, I was back on that field, two years before. We had been playing in Emmaus, Pennsylvania, in a big park, and there were train tracks passing maybe a hundred feet away, parallel to the third base line. As a pitcher, the line of sight was pretty strange, too, because there was a parking lot directly behind the backstop. It was a blindingly sunny, baking-hot day, and a horrible glare was coming off this one white SUV parked right over the umpire's left shoulder.

The grass had just been cut, and the whole place smelled a little bit like onions.

When I came back to reality, I realized Angelika had been clicking away. Also, that she had stopped. "Oh, my God, Pete," she said. "Are you crying?"

8. Slip

It wasn't long after that when I got the first of Grampa's scary phone calls. I was on my way home from school when my cell started vibrating. I assumed it would be AJ, or my mom. Or Angelika. Nobody else ever called me. I made a guess that I was talking to AJ, so I answered, "Sup!"

The phone clicked, and the line went dead. That was a little unusual, but not so crazy. Our town is kind of hilly, so we get a lot of dead spots. I shoved my phone back in my pocket and kept walking. About ten steps later, I felt the buzz again. This time I just said, "Hello?"

There was a long enough pause that I almost hung up. Then I heard Grampa groaning, followed by, "Peter? Peter?"

"Grampa? What's wrong? Are you OK?"

"I . . . I . . . can you come over here?"

Grampa only lived about a mile from our house. "Why? What happened?"

"I fell."

Oh, geez. "Grampa, are you hurt? Let me hang up and call 9-1-1."

"No! I'm not dying. I just fell."

"Let me call my mom. She can get there much faster than —"

"Peter, please — don't tell your mother. Just come over here. Please?"

Grampa never said "please." Twice in one breath had to mean that things were pretty bad. But what was I supposed to do? It's not like they train you for this in Grandparent First Aid 101. "OK, I'm coming," I said. "But it's going to take a while. I'm about a mile and a half from you, and I'm walking."

"Just . . . please . . . hurry."

"Grampa?" I said. But he had already hung up. I started running.

If you ever find yourself a mile and a half away from an emergency, carrying a backpack full of heavy textbooks and camera equipment, that's probably not going to be a good time for you to realize that for the first time in your life, you are woefully out of shape. Within a couple of blocks, I was gasping for air, and my bad arm was throbbing. Every step felt like an eternity, like I was running through Jell-O. The only part of me that was racing successfully was my train of thought. I was in a complete panic. What would I find at my grandfather's house? Was he in a heap at the bottom of his basement stairs? Did he have broken bones? Was he lying in a pool of blood?

I know it couldn't have taken more than fifteen minutes for me to get over there, but I also had time to worry about all the things that could happen in fifteen minutes. Plus, of course, the whole way there I kept thinking, *Call Mom. You have to call Mom. You're a kid. This is too deep for a kid!*

But I never, ever disobeyed Grampa. I kept running.

I didn't know whether my grandfather could make it to the front door, so I went charging around to his back porch, where he had always kept a key hidden under a ceramic planter full of long-dead flowers. My hands were trembling, but I got the key into the door and pushed my way in.

"Grampa?" I shouted.

Nothing.

"GRAMPA?"

Still nothing.

I looked around the whole kitchen, then the living and dining rooms. By this point, I wasn't running. In fact, I was tiptoeing, even though that made no sense. I mean, I knew it was urgent for me to find my grandfather, but I was also terrified of what I would see.

Grampa had to be near a telephone, so I tried to think of where all the extensions were in the house. I realized then that, before my grandmother's death when I was in fifth grade, she had convinced my grandfather to get a phone installed next to the toilet. He had put up a big fight ("Why do we need a special toilet phone? Who do we know that needs an update from *there*?"), but eventually the line had gone in.

I crept up the hallway toward the bathroom, and stuck my head around the doorframe. Grampa was sitting on the floor, with his eyes shut and his back against the wall. There was no blood, which might

have been a good sign. Plus, he was breathing —
loudly. If I could hear his breathing over all of the
gasping and heart pounding that was coming from
me, you knew it had to be loud.

I knelt in front of him, put my good hand on his
shoulder, and said, "Gramp?" I hadn't called him that
since I was little, but somehow the time seemed
right for it. His eyes opened, and for a moment, I got
the feeling he wasn't seeing me at all. Then they sort
of snapped back to life, and he said, "Peter, can you
help me?"

Not "Can you help me up?" Just "Can you
help me?"

This was deeply, deeply not good. How was I supposed to know what to do? I asked if he could move,
and he said, "I think so." With what looked like a lot
of effort, he braced each hand against the floor, then
pulled his legs in so that if he straightened them, he
would be standing up. He added, "I don't know what
happened, but nothing hurts. Can I stand up? I want
to get up." I asked him to lock forearms with me,
and together we managed to get him leaning upright

against the cold tile of the bathroom wall. After a pause there, he was able to walk out, down the hallway, and into his kitchen, where he slumped down in a chair.

I got him a drink — I don't know what a drink was supposed to do, but it seemed like something one might do in a grandfather-rescue-type situation. He gulped it down and asked for a refill, so score one for Peter Friedman, Boy Untrained Paramedic. Then he locked eyes with me and said, "Pete. Don't get old. Don't ever get old."

"Sure," I said. "I'll be sure to step in front of a bus on my sixty-fifth birthday."

He let out a little snort-laugh, and then we just sat there for a while. Eventually, I got myself a water, too; I couldn't believe how wiped out I was just from getting over to Grampa's house. I was really going to have to do something about my fitness in a hurry. Then I asked my grandfather how he had ended up on the floor, and he said, "Slipped."

Yeah, I hadn't really needed a detailed memo to figure that one out. "No," I said, "I mean, why did you slip? Is something" — and here I felt that same stupid lump building up in my throat, just like when I had held the baseball for Angelika — "really wrong with you?"

He sipped some water, and then said, "Peter, sometimes people fall. I'm fine." Then he winced, and added, "Except now my back hurts. Can you go get me some aspirin from the bathroom?"

When I came back with the pills, Grampa's head was slumped forward and his eyes were closed. I put my hand on his shoulder, and he jumped. His head whipped around, and then he said, "Pete — wha — I mean, thanks." He took the aspirin bottle, opened it without fumbling around, got out two tablets, and swallowed them with no problem. But for a moment there, I could have sworn he had been someplace else again.

"Don't look at me like that, Pete. I know how to fall. I fell out of a helicopter under fire in Vietnam — this is nothing. I'm fine."

Was I supposed to believe that? Did *he* believe it?

"And just like I said before, you can't tell your mother about this. She'll just worry, and she has enough on her mind, with bills, and taxes, and jobs, and your sister's college . . ."

"B-but," I stammered, "if there's a problem, you have to tell her. I mean, you *will* tell her, right?"

"I'll make you a deal, Big Man. I promise I'll tell her if I think I'm in any danger, OK?"

I figured that was about as good as it was going to get, so I nodded. I made sure my grandfather didn't need anything else, told him I'd be calling to check on him later, and left. All the way home, I kept thinking how ironic it was that my grandfather, who said he wasn't worried, had begged me not to tell my mom he had fallen. Meanwhile, Mom actually wasn't worried. And me? I was basically having a cow over this.

I remembered something Grampa had said a few days after my grandmother's funeral. We were back at my house, sitting shivah, which is this Jewish ritual where you sit around for a week and everybody comes over to tell you how sorry they are for your loss. By the middle of the week, you aren't really in a total sorrow crisis anymore, and people sort of start chatting normally. Anyway, Samantha and I had been sitting with Grampa, snacking on deli food, and she had asked him if there was anything we could do for him.

"Eat a knish, Sammie."

"No, I mean, can't we do anything to help you?"

He had sighed, rubbed the bridge of his nose, and said, "Sammie, Petey, remember this: There are going to be times in your life when you can't really do anything for anybody. So you might as well eat a knish."

He paused and took a bite of his pastrami on rye sandwich. "What? It's just going to get thrown out."

I guess what I'm trying to say is that Grampa has never been a big fan of accepting help.

When I got home, I felt like a million hours had passed since Grampa's call to my cell phone, but neither of my parents were even home from work yet. I ran upstairs and took a shower, feeling that maybe, just maybe, I could scrub the evidence of what I had seen off my face before dinner. As if my mom would ask. Or believe.

Still, I felt sick all evening. I kept seeing Grampa sitting hunched over on the floor. My legs felt a little weak, and I don't think it was just from the unexpected afternoon sprint. Plus, my elbow was throbbing pretty hard — so hard, I almost popped one of the super-strong postsurgical pain pills I still had in our bathroom cabinet.

So much for joining the track team.

After my parents went to bed, I got online and read up on Alzheimer's disease. The more I read, the more I felt like Angelika had been right. Every single one of the early symptoms matched up with something I'd seen Grampa do. Even though it was late, I called Angelika.

Thankfully, she answered. If I had faced an interrogation from her mom at that point, I think I would have cracked completely. "Angelika?" I said.

"Pete? Hey, hi! I'm so excited! I was just mounting you. I mean, your portrait — you know, with the baseball? I can't wait to hand it in tomorrow. It's really powerful stuff, thanks to you and Adam. I am so going to get an A on this now. The technical values are all there, definitely. Plus, Mr. Marsh is going to fuh-reak over the concept. He was right; once you get that going on, it completely brings a portrait to life. Anyway, I think I really . . . whoa, wait a minute. Am I babbling? I mean, *you* called *me*, right? What's going on?"

I had meant to tell her all about my scary afternoon. Somehow, though, that wasn't what came out of my mouth. "You know, in those pictures . . . I meant to tell you something. I, uh, wasn't really crying. I mean, I had tears. But, um, I just kind of . . . I guess I had a thing. For a minute."

If I had super-hearing, I'm pretty sure I would have been able to hear Angelika's eyebrow arching upward. "Oh, that's fine, then. What a relief. I thought you were totally crying. But if you just had . . . a thing . . . that saves me a lot of trouble."

"Trouble? What do you mean, trouble?"

"See, I've always said I wish I would meet a guy who could actually cry. Because I cry all the time. Remember a few years ago, when President Obama's daughters got their dog? I cried. I cried when my goldfish died — an hour after we bought it. I cry for no reason. I cry for freaking fun! I cry like Lady Gaga changes outfits. So anyway, I swore that if I ever found a crying boy . . ."

"Yeah?"

"Never mind, it doesn't matter. I mean, unless you were actually crying. But you already said it was just a thing. Right?"

"Uh, I might have been crying. A little, tiny bit. One lone, manly tear. So what did you swear you would do?"

"Gee, I'll have to put some thought into this. I promised myself if I met a boy who could totally cry, I'd, like, jump his bones. Smother him in passion. Make him my own. But for one lone, manly tear . . . maybe you should ask me out quick, Peter. You might at least get a kiss out if this, or something."

Holy cow. Ask her out? I had the feeling, like I always did, that she was laughing at me a little. Possibly even toying with me. But she was so pretty. And so smart, and funny, and quick, and my photo partner — this *had* to be my moment.

At these crucial times, some people say, "Carpe diem! Seize the day!" Then they leap right in there and get the girl. Others try to seize the day, but blurt out the worst, most buzz-killing words imaginable. Sadly, I once again proved my knack for being one of the great blurters of the world: "Angelika . . . how did you know your grandmother had Alzheimer's?"

Angelika really was incredible. She changed gears so fast, there wasn't even a pause before she answered. "Oh, boy. Is this why you really called? And here I was, shamelessly flirting with you. What happened today, Pete?"

Dang it, I thought. *What's my problem? Shameless flirting good. Weepy grampa-talk bad.* But I had to keep talking about the situation now that I had brought it up. "My grandfather fell today. He called me and I went running over to his house. When I got there, he seemed kind of disoriented, on and off. But he made me swear I wouldn't tell my parents about it. Now I'm reading all the symptoms online, and he's done, like, half of the things it says to watch for. On the other hand, this one website said that most old people have some of the symptoms, some of the time. So how did you know for sure?"

"Well, first of all, you can't know for sure. Eventually, somebody is going to have to get him to a doctor. And that's really hard. When my grandma got sick, she refused and refused to go."

"Until?"

"Uh, one day, she got in her car and tried to drive to her childhood house. Which was knocked down thirty years ago when they built the old middle school. So she kept driving into the school parking lot, going in circles, then driving back out. Eventually, security noticed, and the police came and stopped her. It was awful. Apparently, she just kept saying, 'Somebody took my house. Why are you arresting me? Why aren't you going after the house thieves?'"

"My grampa hasn't done anything like that yet. But sometimes he just spaces out, and when I look into his eyes, it's like there's nobody home. And he never falls down. This is a man who hikes mountains with a full load of camera gear for fun. And now . . ." I didn't know what was with Angelika and my lump-in-the-throat problems, but at the moment, it seemed kind of like a sleazy way to be racking up points with her.

"All right. Maybe he's losing it and maybe he's not. But, Pete, you have to tell your mother. She's his daughter, right? She's supposed to handle this stuff."

"What about me? I promised I wouldn't tell."

"He shouldn't have made you promise that. It's not fair to you or your mom. And what if he does something really bad, and you could have stopped it by getting your mom involved? How are you going to feel then?"

"Angelika, I'm not a total moron. I made him promise he'd tell my mom if he thought he was in any danger."

"OK, whatever."

"What do you mean, whatever?"

"I mean, the whole point of getting senile is that the person can't think right. His judgment might be impaired. Or maybe he's already forgotten about his whole encounter with you today, and he's sitting around eating bonbons while you're torturing yourself over this. Even though it's not your job. Listen, why don't you sleep on this? Maybe in the morning, you'll feel more like talking to your mom about it."

The worst thing about talking to perceptive people is that they notice everything. But I didn't feel like hearing any more about how wrong I was, so I changed the subject. "I hear you, OK? And I appreciate the advice. Really, I do. Now, can we talk about our next sports assignment? I think we should do the girls' swim meet this Friday, and then the first JV basketball game on Sunday. Mr. Marsh said Linnie Vaughn is going for a record in the backstroke this week, so it would probably be a good idea to get some shots of that for the paper." Linnie Vaughn was the star swimmer at our school. She was also kind of legendarily hot.

Angelika hung right with me on the quick switch. "Sure. Hey, isn't Adam on the JV team?"

"Yeah."

"Maybe we can get a really great shot of him in action, and then blow it up into a poster or something for him."

"Why?"

"Well, because I owe him one. Plus, he has nice eyes. I think they would really pop if we got the right shot. It would be fun to try, anyway."

Suddenly, I felt a flash of jealousy. That's why I said something stupid for the fourth time in, like, twenty minutes. "OK, that's cool. So, can I blow up a shot of Linnie Vaughn?"

She laughed, but it wasn't her usual, merry laugh. I don't know how to explain it, but she sounded kind of sly and angry at the same time as she said, "Sure. I know one thing: You won't have to be a great photographer to make her, um, *features* pop!"

Snap II

Three photos. In the first, a hand holds a baseball in the classic pitcher's grip: first two fingers across the top seam, thumb underneath. The pitcher's arm extends almost straight back into the picture and blurs into his face. The hand and the front of the ball are what photographers refer to as tack sharp: You can see whorls of fingerprint pattern on the skin, a jagged nail, every stitch and scuff on the ball. And you can somehow feel the tension in the fingers, almost imagine that hand crushing yours in its clawed grip. Maybe you've heard somewhere that a pitcher is supposed to hold the ball loosely. Then again, this pitcher isn't going to be throwing the ball anyway.

The second photo is composed exactly like the first, except now the focus is on the middle of the pitcher's arm, so that both the ball and the face are blurred. You can't even read the label on the ball in this one, nor can you be sure the pitcher's eyeglasses are still on his face. What you can't avoid seeing in this one is that elbow: knurled and knotted with scar tissue. The sleeve of the pitcher's Under Armour shirt has been pushed up to his bicep, but you know he must not roll that sleeve back very often. If your elbow looked like his, you'd probably invest in 365 sweaters.

In the third photo, the focus has shifted to the face. The ball is so blurry you can almost see right through it, and the elbow, mercifully, is now smoothed over, stripped of painful detail. The pitcher's eyes are facing forward and slightly down: He may be looking at the ball in his hand. He may be looking at his ruined elbow. His mouth turns down at the corners; his brow is creased in concentrated sorrow. Light catches on a tear that balances on the lower lid of his left eye. You can stare into this face all day, and the eyes are never going to stop their downcast gleaming.

Looking at the three pictures side by side, as they are presented in the photographer's plain black matte frame, you may very well wonder: Who is the subject here? Is he the hand that holds the ball? Is he the scarred and twisted elbow? Could he be neither of these? Could it be that the pitcher will learn to define himself in some brilliant, brave new way? Or is he, in the end, nothing more or less than a sad face behind a blur?

9. the decisive moment

I didn't want Angelika to turn in her three-shot portrait of me. The pictures were incredibly, painfully perfect, which meant Mr. Marsh would probably gather everyone around to *ooh* and *ahh* about them. Can you imagine standing by while a bunch of upperclassmen listen to your teacher say, "See how this tear is sitting there, just waiting to fall? That's genius!" And then he'd probably want to post them in the hallway or something. In which case I'd have to fling myself from a high window.

On second thought, Angelika would probably capture a few good snaps of that action, too.

We were arguing over it when class started that day. She hissed, "I need this grade. And, Pete, you didn't *have* to roll up your sleeve when I asked you to!"

Which was true. But if I hadn't done it, she would have been all mad. Plus, AJ had once told me that, and I quote, "Chicks dig scars. Trust me: It's well-known."

"But it's — look, would you want everyone in the whole world to see *you* looking like that?"

"Like what?" She grinned. "You look really great in the picture . . . strong and manly, yet sensitive. I mean, in real *life* you could use some work, but in the *picture* —"

I sighed. "Can I just see it before class starts?" I asked. She took a flat cardboard mailer out of her backpack, opened it, and slid the three photos out. I grabbed them and held them over my head. She lunged, and you guessed it — once again, Mr. Marsh caught us locked in a full-body embrace.

He said, "When I tell ya that photography should be yer passion, that's not quite how I mean it. Heh-heh." We scrambled to separate, and tumbled into our seats. I tried to be unobtrusive about sliding the pictures over to Angelika, but apparently Houdini doesn't have to feel threatened by my sleight-of-hand skills, because Mr. Marsh came over and said, "Well, well, well. What's this, kids? More of the brilliant work ya somehow manage to create when yer not, um, messin' around?"

Angelika put her hand down on top of the pictures, and said, "It's nothing, Mr. Marsh. I took some pictures, but they're not really ready to be shared, so I'll just —"

"Wait, let me see, Angelika. Ya know I will always tell ya if I think a project needs more work."

"No, I mean they . . . the . . . uh, the subject hasn't given his permission for me to share these yet."

Angelika peeked up at me from under her bangs. For once, it was her turn to blush. Mr. Marsh caught the vibes. "Peter," he said, "you're the subject, right?"

I could feel all the other students' eyes on me as I answered, "Yes, sir."

Mr. Marsh turned to the rest of the group and said, "San Lee, I believe you had a presentation due today — is that correct?" San nodded. Mr. Marsh continued: "And yer presentation was on the photographic style of Henri Cartier-Bresson, yes?" San nodded again. "Then let's table our discussion of Angelika's work until after we have heard from Mr. Lee. I have a feeling he might give us a new perspective on the situation. San? Whaddaya got?"

San roused himself from his usual lounging position, and made his way to the front with a set of prints and a laptop computer. When he was all set up, he started a slide show, and three words were projected onto our room's overhead screen:

THE DECISIVE MOMENT

Then San clicked through a series of black-and-white photos: Three women doing each other's hair. A couple kissing on top of a tower in Paris. An old woman sitting at a sidewalk cafe, giving a beautiful younger woman a dirty look. A crush of people getting off a ship, with a crying man in the middle, hugging an elderly lady. Each picture was almost too private to look at, yet here they were, on display in our classroom, probably fifty years after some of their subjects had died of old age.

San spoke: "Henri Cartier-Bresson was a French photographer who started becoming well-known in the 1930s. He practically invented the art of street photography. He would walk along, with his Leica camera — just one fifty-millimeter lens, no zoom — and snap pictures of whatever he saw that interested him. He tried not to get the attention of his subjects. He even taped over the shiny parts of his camera with black electrical tape so that the camera wouldn't be as noticeable. In 1952, he published a book of his work, titled *Images à la Sauvette*, which literally means something like 'images on the run' or 'stolen images.' But in English, the book became known as *The Decisive Moment*. When I look at his work, I can see how the images are all three things: stolen, taken on the run, and decisive. There's also a kind of Zen to the pictures, because he only had one shot to capture that exact, unposed instant. Of course, he was working with an old-fashioned film camera, so he couldn't just put it in burst mode and go click, click, click eight times a second. And the instant before or after the one he caught probably wouldn't have been as perfect."

He paused then to pin up his own photos.

"Can ya tell us about these, San?" Mr. Marsh asked.

"Sure. I decided to imitate Cartier-Bresson by walking through the hallways of our school with my camera and one fifty-millimeter lens. I used the swivel viewfinder on my camera so I could shoot from my waist, and didn't use a flash or burst mode. I also didn't do any retouching or Photoshopping, because Cartier-Bresson was all about the shot. He didn't care about the developing process. Anyway, here's what I got."

The first photo San pointed to was taken in the stairwell of the building. A really skinny guy was facing the camera, on his way up the steps, and you could see that the shoulder of a huge guy going down had just bumped him pretty hard. The skinny guy was grimacing, but you could tell he was going to keep walking.

The next shot showed the view down a nearly empty hallway: two parallel walls of lockers seemed to go on forever into the distance. There were only two people in sight. In the background, a custodian was bent over his push broom. In the foreground, a girl was throwing a gum wrapper over her shoulder.

San's third and final picture showed a wide view of the front entrance to the school on a sunny day, looking straight on at the four steel doors. There were four people sitting on the cement stairs, facing the camera. On the left, a guy and a girl were clearly arguing over something. His mouth was open, and he looked really angry. She was turned partly away from him and was raising her palm toward him in the classic tell-it-to-the-hand position. On the right, two guys were sitting with their arms around each other, goofy smiles on their faces, looking completely engrossed in each other.

He turned to Mr. Marsh, who said, "So, Mr. Lee, can ya tell me the essence of whatcha were trying to capture here?"

San looked right at me and said, "The truth. I think the best use for a camera is to capture the truth."

Meanwhile, I was thinking, *Great! So just because some French dude shot a bunch of embarrassing photos of random strangers sixty years ago, now I'm supposed to let Angelika hand in a gigantic blowup poster of me crying like a four-year-old? And of course the funny part is, we have no idea what those poor suckers thought about the pictures. For all we know, they all jumped off the Eiffel Tower right after the book came out.*

I looked down and spent some time picking at the frayed hem of my left pant leg.

"So, guys, whadda the rest of ya think? Is photography all about telling the troot?"

I had to speak up. "Well, my grandfather was a professional photographer, and he said his job was to present his subjects the way they would *want* to be seen."

Angelika said, "But your grandfather shot weddings. That's different. San was going for more of a photojournalism thing. Right?"

San nodded.

"OK, then," I said. "What about beauty? Isn't photography an art form? And shouldn't art be beautiful?"

Danielle chimed in. I'd figured she would, being the layout editor of the yearbook and all. "I think sometimes a piece of art can be beautiful because of the way the elements in it are arranged. Even if the individual elements aren't pretty, they can make a beautiful whole. That's why I like doing layouts so much. It's all about the composition."

Danny said, "I think there's no right answer. Sometimes a photo is for truth, sometimes it's for beauty, and sometimes . . . it's for something else."

"Something else?" San asked. "What else is there?"

There was a long pause then, which lasted until I blurted out, "Doesn't the subject get a say in how the photo gets used? I mean, what if that kid who got his shoulder banged into is embarrassed about it? Or what if one of those people from the front steps has, like, a religious objection to being photographed? Is everything and everyone fair game?"

Don't you hate it when teachers act like they're talking about one thing, but really they're twisting the direction of the conversation so they can make a point about something totally different? Mr. Marsh said, "That's debatable in a public place like a school, where the subjects haven't consented to having their pictures taken. But I think there's an implied contract when someone agrees to pose for a portrait — like in the case of Peter and Angelika. Don't'cha agree, Angelika?"

Wow, the only thing worse than the conversation-twisting gambit is when the teacher completely puts a student on the spot. Angelika kind of squirmed, picked a hangnail, and said, "I don't know. I guess . . . I mean, I kind of ambushed Peter with . . . um . . . an object so I could get his reaction on film. And he didn't agree to that in advance, because he didn't know I was going to do it. Obviously. So I think it should be up to him."

Mr. Marsh said, "Well, Peetuh?"

I generally try to be patient with people, but this was starting to get me mad. "Do we really have to discuss this in the middle of class? Now even if I don't say yes, I've already been dragged over the coals in front of everybody."

Mr. Marsh said, "Sorry, Peetuh. Yer right. I just got all excited to have a real-life example of an ethical argument popping up right before my eyes. You can totally do whatever ya need to do with the pictures." Then he winked. He actually freaking winked. Ugh. "And who knows what might, uh, come up if you two have another session together?"

Angelika said, "I'm sorry, too, Pete. I wasn't trying to . . . uh, well . . . Look, I'll destroy the prints and delete the files, OK? It's not worth all this."

I looked at the prints that were still on the table between Angelika and me. They *were* really good. Then I looked at Angelika. She was looking right back at me, and her eyes just seemed so sad all of a sudden. I sighed, and slid the portraits across the table into her hand. "Hand 'em in," I said. I still wasn't too sure I wanted the whole world to see them, but on the other hand, they definitely captured some kind of moment of truth. And if the truth was good enough for Henri Cartier-Bresson, I supposed it was good enough for me.

San stopped on the way back to his seat and patted me on the shoulder. Mr. Marsh smiled, and swept the photos out of Angelika's hand. The class burst into semi-mocking applause. And my ears turned really, really red.

But on the way out of class, Angelika bumped her hip against mine and smiled.

10. cutting class

For a while there, you'd almost think I'd totally adjusted to my new life as a nonathlete whose childhood idol was slipping down the tubes. I mean, for a couple of weeks, life almost rocked: Angelika and I were bonding — and not just flirty-bonding, but really talking about life stuff. I was still clueless about how to make a move with her, but I figured if I just stood close enough to her, for long enough, eventually we'd accidentally stumble into an empty Hebrew school classroom or something. I talked with Grampa on the phone a couple of times, plus I stopped by his house one day unannounced, and each time, he seemed to be on topic and focused. Plus, I was even getting semi-popular at school.

With my new sports-photographer gig, whenever a new biweekly issue of the school newspaper came out, at least one person would always come up to me and compliment me on my work. Then this one issue came out with two of my shots on the back page: one was AJ poised in the air for a slam dunk, and the other was the super-hot Linnie Vaughn arched halfway backward in the air, pushing off at the start of a backstroke race. I was sitting at lunch with AJ that day, and tons and tons of people came over to high-five him.

This one guy we knew from middle school walked up to our table and said, "AJ — that was such a cool picture of you in action. You are the *man!*"

AJ said, "Thanks, Tim. It was no big deal. I was just playing my game. Pete did all the work. I mean, he's the one that took the picture."

Tim glanced over at me, clearly not impressed. "Uh, that's cool," he muttered.

"AND he took that suh-mokin' picture of Linnie Vaughn," AJ added.

Now I had Tim's attention. "Really? You took that picture, too? That one is awesome! I'm totally going to put it up in my locker!"

Some random kid walking past stopped and said,

142

"You're the guy who gave the world Linnie Vaughn in a bathing suit? In color? Dude. I'm in awe. Thank you!"

Well, that was awkward. Is it better to be ignored, or to be the hero of hormonally challenged geeks everywhere? Anyway, when it was just me and AJ again, he said, "By the way, thanks. I'm hoping the varsity coach might notice me, and he's gotta see that picture around, right? I know I still have to build up my stats, get more playing time, work on my D — but every little bit helps."

He stopped to take a huge bite of his pizza, then gulped it down and said, "You know, hoops is cool and all. But what I really can't wait for is baseball. You and me, together again, showing everyone what we can do — it's gonna be sick. Sick! Hey, only a few more months, right? Then you can get in *front* of the camera for a while!"

I didn't say anything; I just kept chewing my extremely greasy pork barbecue sandwich. It was one of those times when I'm really glad AJ never notices whether I reply or not. He rambled on, through another round of guys stopping by, some additional Linnie Vaughn innuendo, a thorough dissection of his basketball season to date, and finally . . . mercifully . . . the bell.

Speaking of dissection, it was a dissection lab in biology class that smacked me back to reality. My bio teacher was an ancient crone named Mrs. Singley, who knew a ton about the subject and was a pretty entertaining speaker. Unfortunately, she was also kind of blind and deaf, which meant that labs got a bit out of hand. Imagine a room full of nervous freshmen with scalpels, smelly dead animals soaking in formaldehyde, very little supervision, and thirty other freshmen to impress, and you kind of get the idea of how those sessions went.

This was a pretty major lab. We had already cut up worms, fish, and frogs, but today was Mammal Day. I walked in from my lunch with AJ, and found fifteen preserved fetal pigs in sealed plastic bags, one on each table in the room. My partner was a kid named Matt, who had the same kind of oblivious charm that made AJ so beloved by all. He was also immensely hyper, which didn't bother me most days but wasn't so comforting when he had a razor-sharp scalpel in hand.

Mrs. Singley gave us some basic directions and handed out the packet we all had to fill out. Then she stepped aside and let us start slicing up our piggies. "Dude," Matt said as he started using a bone scissors to split open the rib cage of our unfortunate new pet. "D'you think they purposely planned this for a day when we were having pork for lunch? Because, I mean, I could see getting really nauseated if you thought about that too hard. Not that I plan to think about it much. Oops, watch out for the bloody fluid there! Wow, who knew one pig could be so, um, drippy? Anyway, check out this stringy part here behind the ribs. I think that would have made one tasty sandwich niblet, don't you? Hey, hand me a pencil. I think we're supposed to draw this artery thing here. Ugh, I got some guts on the handout. Could you do me a favor and just wipe that off? Or maybe we should switch places for a while. You have to be neater than I am."

So we switched places. I was a pretty good pig eviscerator, too. I cut out the heart with no problems. The lungs followed. The liver? Check. The stomach. The intestines. The undeveloped reproductive system. Check, check, check. But then Mrs. Singley stopped everybody.

"Excuse me, class, but I seem to have left a page out of the packet. The last thing you need to do is dissect one forelimb of your pig and draw a detailed diagram of the elbow joint. . . ."

Suddenly, I felt light-headed. I staggered a couple of steps sideways, and somehow managed to stop gagging long enough to ask Matt to take over for me. He stepped in, grabbed up the tools, and started cutting. Which I might have been OK with, but of course the operation came with narration:

"Hey, hi! Wave to our friends, piggie! Good job, piggie!"

"Uh, Matt," I said, trying not to retch, "do you think we could just, like, get the work done? There's not much time left in the period, and —"

"Don't worry, Pete. I can bond with our piglet and

work at the same time. Hey, Pigster, I like the way your joint articulates when you wave! Look how nicely your ulna and radius pivot together! Pete, check this out! If I pull his arm back, it's almost like he's getting ready to throw a ball or something. Just . . . gotta . . . get it back a little . . . farther —" I heard a sickening wet snap. "Oopsie! Guess Porky here is out for the season!"

I felt a lurch in my gut, and instantly, my mouth was full of half-digested pig parts.

I almost made it to the door.

By the time the mess was cleaned up, I was in the nurse's office. I kind of felt better — at least physically — after my massive projectile hurling spasm, but I played it up like I was dying so I wouldn't have to go back to class and see people. So the nurse called my mom, but my mom couldn't come to get me. Naturally, my dad was away on business, which left only one relative in town: Grampa. The nurse called him, and he said he would keep me at his house until my parents got home from work.

I climbed into Grampa's huge Goldberg Photo SUV, which he had always needed for hauling around his cameras, lights, tripods, backdrops, and assorted other tools of the trade. Now, with nothing in the back, it felt cavernously hollow inside. I was on the edge of my seat, waiting for him to blank out, swerve off the road, and smash me into a tree. Grampa had always been a fairly impatient driver, so I could only imagine how scary he would be if his mind was going. He was in total control, though. In fact, he was alert enough to grill me about what had happened.

I told him the whole lab story, and then he said, "So, forget about your stomach troubles. What I really want to know is, how are things going with your new girlfriend, whatshername?"

"She's not my girlfriend, Grampa," I said, gritting my teeth as he slowed down at the last minute for a red light. "Her name is Angelika. But she's just my partner in photography class."

"Partner, huh? Promising."

"No, we didn't even choose each other."

"But she modeled for you. Photographers and models: I've seen it a million times. I could tell you stories from my younger days. . . ."

Between Grampa's famously heavy accelerator foot, my pig experience, and now the thought of my grandparent having a love life, I was about to roll down my window and heave. But when I actually turned to look out the window, I noticed that we had completely driven past Grampa's house. "Uh, Grampa? Where are we going?"

He looked almost scared for a second, but then recovered so fast you almost could have missed the whole thing. "Oh, I just wanted to stop by the drug-store and get you some Pepto-Bismol. Why?"

Pretty smooth cover-up, Grampa, I thought.

When we got to his house, he set me up on the couch with a pillow, a blanket, and a remote control, and told me I could nap or watch TV — whatever I wanted. "Where are you going?" I asked.

"Out. Now get some rest," he said. I tried to press him for details, but he just shrugged me off and walked out of the house. I flicked on the TV, and channel surfed for as long as I could stand it. I was incredibly thirsty and had the world's single worst pig-barf-and-formaldehyde aftertaste in my mouth, so eventually I was forced to get out from my couch-nest and make my way down the hall to the bathroom. I splashed some water in my face, brushed my teeth with a finger, and then noticed something I hadn't seen before. There were Post-it notes all over the place. Next to the toothbrush holder, a yellow note said, in shaky block letters, "BRUSH AM + PM." On the top of the toilet tank, there was a hot-pink one: "FLUSH!"

I went into the kitchen for a glass of juice and found the same scenario there. Grampa had notes to remind him to turn off the oven, the stove, and the coffee-maker. There was even a note posted behind the toaster oven with directions for making toast. This scared me. My grandfather had been cooking his own meals for as long as I could remember — and now he needed step-by-step instructions for heating bread?

I heard the rattly click of Grampa's key in the front door, and scrambled back to the couch. I covered myself all up with the blanket and pretended to sleep. Really, I thought there was no way I could take a nap while I was so freaked out by the dissection and worried about my grandfather and his newly annotated existence. But somehow I dozed off, because the next thing I knew, my mother was bent over me with her hand on my forehead.

"Mom, I'm fine," I said. "I just got a little sick before, but I'm all better now."

Mom gave me her special don't-question-the-doctor look — not that she's actually a doctor, but she definitely picked up the look from somewhere. "Peter, the school nurse said you looked awful. I believe the exact phrase was, 'Your son's face is the color of oatmeal.' I was worried all afternoon, and now you say you're fine? I don't know: I think you'd better stay home tomorrow."

"Whatever. But I'm telling you, I don't have some funky virus or anything. I just ate a really disgusting lunch and then . . . well, there was this pig . . . and . . . can I just tell you the whole thing later?"

She nodded.

"And besides," I added, "who says that being the color of oatmeal is a bad thing? Maybe the nurse meant it in a flattering way. I mean, oatmeal is a delicious, low-fat food, rich in fiber. In fact, I've heard that eating oatmeal actually lowers your bad cholesterol."

She rolled her eyes and prodded me off the couch. "OK, Mr. Handsome Oatmeal Face. Go say thank you to your grandfather."

I found Grampa in the bathroom, just standing there. At first, I thought he must have been in one of his spaced-out trances, but then I noticed what he was holding in one hand: a bunch of Post-its. I realized then why I hadn't seen any little notes around his house before: He must have been in the habit of taking them down every time we were supposed to come over. We almost never showed up unannounced there, and the one time I had recently — when he had fallen down — I hadn't exactly been conducting a home inspection.

Anyway, Grampa noticed me looking at his handful of little papers, and held the pointer finger of his other hand to his lips. "Shhh," he said, and winked. I gulped and nodded. What else was I supposed to do? He gave me a brief, fierce hug, and pushed me toward the door.

On the way home, Mom asked, "Hey, did everything go all right with your grandfather today? I know you've been worried about him lately, but he seemed fine to me just now."

Well, at least I could tell the complete truth in response to that. "He sure did, Mom!" I said, forcing myself to smile. "So, what's for dinner?"

"Ham," she replied.

11. my old friend the blues

That night, after I had (barely) survived my third dead-pig encounter of the day, done all my homework, and fielded the obligatory phone calls from Angelika ("Ooh, Peter, are you all right? Because Linnie Vaughn is going to be really bummed if you, like, die. . . .") and AJ ("Dude, did you really hurl all over the classroom door? I heard it was pretty graphic!"), I sat up in bed for hours.

Have you ever looked around your room and suddenly noticed something about your decorations that's never hit you before? Because it happened to me that night: I realized that almost everything that mattered to me in there had come from my grandfather. He had painted the walls in Yankee pinstripes as a surprise for my seventh birthday. Then he had taken me to a game, and brought along a gigantic telephoto lens and his super-professional wide-angle one, too. That's why I had huge blowup prints of Derek Jeter, Mariano Rivera, and Jorge Posada on one wall, and an even bigger one of the view from the upper deck on another. As if that weren't enough, he had also taken the family portrait on my dresser and bought me the airplane models that lined the top of my bookcase.

Plus, half of the books were from him. And a bunch of old rhythm and blues CDs that he had probably made me listen to a million times in his truck, and then finally given to me when I happened to mention one day that one of them had a couple of catchy songs on it. Believe it or not, although I wouldn't have admitted it to friends or anything, I had actually copied every single track of those CDs onto my hard drive.

I had to be the only teenager in America who owned the complete recordings of Ray Charles AND B. B. King. In a strange mood just then, I found the Ray Charles collection on the MP3 player next to my bed (yet another Grampa gift), and pressed PLAY. Even at low, midnight volume, Ray's gravelly voice filled every inch of the room:

"You know the night time, darling, is the right time,
To be with the one you love, now . . ."

Which goes to show you how incredibly depressing it is to listen to music when you have insomnia. I mean, pretty much by definition, if you're under the age of seventy, and you're listening to a fifty-year-old recording in the middle of the night, you are obviously not curled up with the one you love. Unless the one you love happens to be either as geeky as you, or deaf. Of course, AJ always says there's no such thing as love anyway. In his poetic words, "It's all just hormones, my friend. You might as well just say you're in testosterone with somebody. And if you're really lucky, she might be in estrogen with you."

But anyway, my thoughts shifted from worrying about my grandfather to wondering what Angelika was up to. Sleeping, probably. But maybe not. Maybe she was sitting in her own room, in front of her computer screen, looking at pictures of me. Maybe she was, at that very moment, hoping I'd get over my stomach problem and come back to school in the morning. Possibly, she was even thinking about what I'd be wearing, what we would talk about, whether we would get to work together in class.

Because I was wondering all those things about her. I even found myself wondering whether she would have her hair down in front of her glasses, or tucked behind one ear. I liked it both ways.

It hit me, at 1:23 A.M.: *I am in testosterone with Angelika.*

Yeah, I know. Duh. But it really, really hit me. This wasn't just flirting, or playing around, or wanting a girlfriend. This was Peter Friedman wanting Angelika Stone. In pretty much every sense of the word. I wanted to know her. I wanted to be with her. I wanted to tell her everything about me, and still have her want to hear more. I wanted to introduce her to Ray Charles and hope she liked him.

My second-to-last thought before I finally nodded off was *I need to find a way to be alone with Angelika*. That was immediately followed by *But how? There's never a good bar mitzvah around when you need one.*

As you might expect, I got teased for days about the bio lab fiasco, until finally I was saved when some other kid slipped in the lunch line and dumped a tray of chicken pot pie all over a cafeteria lady. But things got back to normal, and life was swimming along again until the day we started our next photography project. Mr. Marsh got so pumped up by San's Henri Cartier-Bresson project that he decided the whole class's next assignment would be to walk around the school taking candids for the yearbook — with no flash, no zoom, and nothing but a 50mm lens.

A couple of the seniors squawked about this, because apparently, the usual method of getting the so-called candids was for the upperclassmen to run around shooting posed pictures of huge groups of their friends. But Mr. Marsh stood firm: Each of us had exactly one week to take ten really good unposed pictures, and as he put it, "They bettuh not be pickchuhs a' yer friends. 'Cause ya better believe I'm gonna know."

Angelika and I were cruising down the hall to class the next day, with our school-issued cameras around our necks — because there was no way I would expose Grampa's equipment to the war zone of my school's hallways — when it happened. I stopped to snap a shot of a teacher yelling at some couple that had just been displaying what our student handbook refers to as "undue physical affection." Just as we started walking again, Linnie Vaughn came up to me.

Linnie Vaughn! Came up to me!

Ahem. Anyway, she came up to me and said, "Hey, you're the kid who took the picture of me for the paper."

I didn't trust myself to speak, so I just swallowed and nodded.

She reached out and punched me in the right shoulder. Apparently, swimmers are strong, because it hurt: I was just lucky she hadn't nailed my bad arm. Then she said, "Great job!"

I swallowed and nodded some more. Linnie turned to Angelika and said, "He's so cute! Does he talk?"

Angelika said, "Uh, once in a while. But a lot of times he just stands in one place and drools like this."

Linnie Vaughn chuckled. "Well," she said, "when he recovers, can you ask if he's going to take pictures at regionals this Saturday night? There's going to be a victory party afterward at my house, and it would be so cool to have a photographer there!"

I stood in one place. And probably drooled a little.

Angelika said, "What if you don't win?"

"Funny girl," Linnie replied. "We'll win."

"Great!" Angelika said. "Can I come, too? Usually we don't let this kid go out in public without a mute-to-English translator."

Linnie said, "Sure. Just make sure he makes me look good, OK?"

I think I managed a nod and a squeak. Linnie turned sharply and walked away, as Angelika bumped me with her hip. I didn't know exactly what had happened, but it felt kind of like I had just witnessed two lionesses marking their territory. "Pete, are you going to say something? Ever again?"

I thought, *Be cool. Be cool! What would AJ say in this situation?* "Uh," I blurted in what I hoped was a slightly suave manner. "Do you have a date for Linnie's party?"

"Nope," she said. "Why? Are you asking me?"

I nodded. After its brief interlude of functionality, my throat had locked up again.

Angelika smiled, put her hand on my elbow, and started guiding me toward the photo lab. "Absolutely, Pete," she said. "I'd love to be your date!"

We turned a corner into a much noisier hallway, which cut off the conversation for a moment. But I could have sworn I heard Angelika mutter, "Like I was going to let you go alone . . ."

I walked home with AJ that day, and he was bouncing around the sidewalk like a man possessed. "Buddy boy," he said, "this party is going to be the sickest party ever."

As he ran across a street against the red light, I muttered, "You said 'party' twice in that sentence."

Somehow he heard, because when he got to the far side of the street, he said, "Party! Party! Party! It bears repeating, my friend. Think upon this: Linnie Vaughn invited you to a party, a fest, a fiesta, a soiree. Wait, a soiree is a kind of party, right? I, uh, just kind of threw that one in. But I'm getting a sixty-eight in French, so . . ."

"Yeah, AJ, it's a kind of party. But —"

"Soiree! Soiree! Soiree! So, are you going to, like, get all busy with Angelika? Because she's your date and all . . . but then again, Linnie Vaughn is Linnie Vaughn."

"Which means?"

"She's the Queen of Hotness. And she invited you to her party specifically. AND she has a thing for younger guys."

"What are you talking about? Who in the world told you that?"

"Dude, it's known."

Him and his *It's known.* "Well, it doesn't matter. I've been thinking about it a lot, and I definitely think I like Angelika."

AJ punched me in the shoulder, exactly where Linnie Vaughn had. It occurred to me that maybe he should go after her if she really liked younger guys. I mean, they shared the same taste in punching bags, anyway. That had to be worth something. "That's what I'm talkin' about!" he yelled in my ear as he jumped over a garbage can in the middle of the sidewalk. "Go get her, little tiger! Rrrawr! Oh, this is going to be sick, sick, sick! And don't worry if you get nervous at the party about, uh, seduction procedures. Fortunately for you, my friend, I have also been invited to this shindig."

Whoa. It was strange enough that one of us had been invited to Linnie's party, but what were the chances that *both* of us had been? Admittedly, AJ was a popular jock, but this was *Linnie Vaughn's* party — the pinnacle of cool happening-ness. I looked at AJ blankly.

"What?" he said. "Isn't 'shindig' another word for

party? Because if not, my eighth-birthday invitations made no sense whatsoever."

I sighed. AJ could just be so tiring. It was like having a puppy that followed you to school. A huge, overly friendly, hyper puppy that could talk. And talk. And talk. "Yes, a shindig is a party. I'm just trying to figure out how you got yourself invited."

"Well, the whole team is going to be there."

"What whole team?"

"The JV basketball team. This is going to be an excellent networking opportunity for you. I mean, four of those guys are baseball players, too. I've been telling them how cool you are and everything, but they really need to hang out with you so the team can start to gel before the season gets going. There's Ray, the shortstop; DJ, the right fielder; Tommy — you remember Tommy? From two years ago in All-Star Baseball Academy? Hey, are you even listening? Here I am, trying to get you back on the path to awesomeness, and you're staring into space like I'm not even making any sense."

"AJ, tryouts are still three months away."

"Ah, but it's never too early to work on team chemistry. Speaking of chemistry, I can't wait to hang out with Angelika and you at the same time. I need to observe your interactions in detail."

"Why?"

"Duh. Because, as your wingman and personal hormonal advisor, I have to analyze your moves, her countermoves, your counter-countermoves, her counter-counter-countermoves. . . . Wow, this is really complicated stuff. Maybe we should stop by Staples on the way home so I can buy a clipboard and some graph paper."

"AJ, I appreciate all of this," I said. "But isn't there a chance I might actually have things under control on my own?"

He looked at me for a second, and then busted out laughing. I took that as a "NO!"

12. the longest day

I don't know what other people like to do to get psyched up for a big party night, but my approach was to have brunch with my grandfather. We had a long-standing Saturday-morning tradition of going to a diner together once in a while, and it had definitely been a while. Plus, there's nothing like checking my favorite person for signs of dementia to get me in the mood to rock and roll. Actually, smacking my head repeatedly with a heavy shovel would have been just about as much fun. But at least with this option, I got hash browns.

He picked me up right on time, and when I got in the car, he seemed to be in a great mood. I told him about my sports shooting progress, the party that night, and our Henri Cartier-Bresson assignment.

"Sounds like this Mr. Marsh really knows his stuff," Grampa said.

"Yeah, I'm learning a ton in his class," I said.

"Good. Are you going to shoot at the party tonight?"

"Nah."

"Why not? You're going to have your camera on you anyway, right? You're going there straight from the meet."

"But —"

"You could get some great candids there. And people love getting their pictures taken at parties."

I thought about what I had heard about high school parties. Somehow, I didn't think people would necessarily be overjoyed if some freshman was getting up in their faces and recording their lusty, potentially illegal escapades. Plus, I didn't want to be thinking about a school project at the party — I wanted to concentrate on getting closer with Angelika. Besides, I would probably need to focus some of my energy on keeping AJ from embarrassing me too much. "I'll think about it, OK?" I said.

He nodded, and then we didn't talk anymore until we had gotten to the diner and slid into our favorite booth. I ordered the Big Man Breakfast, which was a gigantic platter of eggs, pancakes, and every variety of greasy meat you can jam onto an oversize plate. Grampa grunted, "Guess your stomach is better," then put in his order for a bagel with lox and a cup of coffee.

Our food came out pretty quickly, and it all tasted excellent. Everything was going great until a beautiful, blonde-haired, youngish lady came over and got Grampa's attention. "Hey, you're Paul Goldberg, aren't you?"

He looked up from his bagel, nodded, and smiled, but I could tell he didn't know who this woman was.

"I'm Anna McGuire. You were my wedding photographer. Two years ago? At the Lehigh Country Club? You did a fabulous job! We love our photos — we look at them all the time! Anyway, I just wanted to stop by and, uh, say hi."

Grampa kept smiling and nodding for a beat too long without saying anything. Then, finally, he said,

"It's nice to meet you!" Anna McGuire didn't know what to say to that, so she just kind of stammered and stutter-stepped backward, away from our table and out the door.

This was bad. It was so, so bad. Remember how I mentioned that his number one motto had always been "Get the shot"? Well, his number two motto was "Never, EVER forget a bride's name." When you've spent forty years as a wedding photographer in one little valley, you meet brides all the time whose weddings you've shot. I mean, this happened to Grampa at least every other time he went out in public. And in my entire life, I had never seen him blank out on a bride. This time, not only had he blanked out on the bride's name — he had pretty much forgotten how to interact completely.

"Gramp," I said. "Are you all right?"

"Why wouldn't I be?" he asked, taking a huge bite of bagel.

"Well, that lady that just came to the table. You didn't seem to know who she —"

"Peter, what are you talking about? We were just

sitting here having a little conversation about . . . about . . . about things. And now you've gotten yourself all in an uproar. Everything's fine. Eat your food."

"But —"

"It'll get cold." He looked away from me, and spent the next few minutes elaborately refilling, creaming, and sugaring his coffee. He seemed totally calm, as though he had already forgotten all about his failed conversation with the woman. But I didn't see how that could be possible.

"Hey, Grampa," I said. "Have you ever forgotten a bride?"

"No," he said, "never! I've made some big mistakes in my career . . . like this one time, I forgot to bring extra film for my cameras and had to run out to a drugstore between the ceremony and the reception. I thought the groom's father was going to have a coronary! And another time, I showed up at Our Lady of Mercy when the wedding was supposed to be at Our Lady of *Infinite* Mercy. But I can still remember every single bride I ever shot."

"Every single one?"

"Sure. Watch this! December 3, 1972: Bethany Winmoor. October 5, 1987: LeeAnn Dalrymple. March 6, 1994: Erin Kopesky."

"How about Anna McGuire? Did you ever shoot a wedding for someone named Anna McGuire?"

He took a sip of his coffee, then said, "Blonde? Pretty?" I nodded. "Sure, I remember her. My main Nikon was in the shop, and I shot her whole wedding with one of my backups. That was back in . . . I think it was in . . . June, maybe? Two, three years ago? I don't know — something like that. Hmm, I wonder how she's doing. Funny that I've never seen her around. Why do you ask?"

The hair stood up on the back of my neck: Grampa had just completely missed several minutes of his life. "Oh, nothing," I said. "More coffee?"

I spent the rest of the afternoon obsessing about Alzheimer's disease, and looking again at all the websites I'd found about it. *Was* my grandfather losing his memory? Deep down, I just freaking knew he had to be, but that didn't mean I knew what to do about it. One of the sites I found was all about how an elderly person's children are supposed to step in and make the decisions about care. My mom was his only child, and she didn't want to listen to what I'd already said. Plus, Grampa didn't want me to tell her anything more, and besides, Grampa had never let anybody make any decisions about his life.

I remembered this one time, maybe a year after my grandmother's death, Mom had suggested that maybe it was time for Grampa to think about going out on dates with other women. He responded by throwing the only cursing fit I had ever seen from him, kicking our whole family out of his house, and then sitting down to cry at his kitchen table while I watched through the little window in his front door. Mom never brought it up again, and Grampa never went out on any dates.

One thing was for sure: Even if Mom did start to believe, helping Grampa wasn't going to be easy.

Eventually, it was time to leave for the swim meet, so Mom and I got in the car. When we were something like half a mile from home, I realized I had forgotten to bring my best indoor-sports lens, so I asked her to turn around and go back for it. Then, of course, I started arguing with myself for the millionth time:

So, Grampa forgot one bride's face. One bride out of hundreds. Thousands, probably. So what? I just forgot to bring the single most important item for a shoot. Does that make me senile? And Mom forgets the title of every song she's ever heard — it drives Dad and me nuts. But I'm not building a case for shipping her off to a home. Plus, Samantha drove all the way back to college last month without her cell phone. Her cell phone! That's like me forgetting to bring my left arm or something. But I didn't think she was losing it.

On the other hand, none of us had given away our prize possessions because we knew we couldn't use them correctly anymore. I mean, geez, I still had my favorite Stealth baseball bat hanging in its bag in the garage, even though I knew I would never be able to play ball again. That was what made me feel the worst for Grampa: If he had given away his cameras, he must have known what was going on. What was it like for him, spending most of his time alone, and working frantically to hide the whole problem whenever anybody was around?

By the time I got done agonizing over all of this, Mom had pulled up to the school. I thought about asking her to park and then telling her about Grampa's fall, the spacing-out times he was having — everything. But I was running late because of the lens issue, *and* I was kind of dying to see Angelika, *and* the meet was about to start.

What would Grampa have done in this situation? Would he have made himself late to the meet in order to tell Mom about all this stuff? I heard his voice the way I always did when I was unsure, and it told me what he had always said: "Get the shot. You've gotta get the shot!" Maybe that was just me giving myself permission to do what I wanted to do anyway, but I went with it. I kissed Mom on the cheek, grabbed my camera bag, and jumped out of the car.

Angelika was already set up by the side of the pool. She didn't even look up from her light meter when I came in, but I think I did get a "hey" out of her. *Wow, this is going to be some rockin' date*, I thought. I knelt down next to her and started taking out my stuff. "OK," Angelika said, "I have a game plan. I copied the swim team roster, and crossed out all the girls we got shots of last time. Here's a list of who's left." She looked up and smiled at me then. *Aha*, I thought. *Guess I won't be focusing on Linnie Vaughn this evening.*

A few minutes later, Linnie actually came and stood over us. She had already swum a few warm-up laps, and she was soaking wet. "Hi, guys," she said. "All ready to party later?" Looking up at her, I tried really hard to avoid staring at her body. Which meant I forced myself to look straight up at her face. I couldn't help but notice that her teeth were super-white. I mean, crazy super-white. Like, visible-from-space white. Linnie Vaughn should have been the poster girl for Crest or something. I wondered whether she had ever had braces, because aside from their laserlike gleam, those teeth were also laser-straight. I hoped my staring wasn't as obvious as it felt.

Angelika shifted her tripod a little, so that one of the legs came down on my toe — hard. Oopsie. So much for the not-obvious-staring thing. "Uh, what can we do for you, Linnie?" I squeaked.

Linnie stepped even closer to me — and she had already been uncomfortably close. Now she was close enough to drip on my feet. "Just make me look beautiful," she said.

"No worries," Angelika said brightly. "We're not here to get more pictures of you, Linnie. Pete got so many great ones of you last time that now we can just concentrate on the rest of the team."

Linnie looked down at my feet, then back at Angelika. "Ooh, sorry," she said. "I think I just got your boyfriend all wet." Then she walked away.

The silence that followed was, like, the absolute definition of "awkward." I tried really hard to wipe the chlorinated droplets off my sneakers unobtrusively while I formatted the memory card in my camera and slipped in a new battery. Deep in the cushioned interior of Grampa's old camera bag, wa-a-ay in the bottom of the spare-battery compartment,

I found an unopened container of Tic Tacs. That was typical: Grampa had always stashed breath mints all over the place. He said there's nothing worse than a wedding photographer with rancid breath.

I figured I could use a burst of minty freshness, so I popped open the pack and slipped a Tic Tac into my mouth. When I finally dared to face Angelika again, I held out the case and said, "Breath mint?"

She just kind of growled as she took one. The swimming started, and I felt like we were sitting in some kind of Chamber of Silence in the middle of the crowded pool deck. She said nothing. I matched her wordless for wordless. Her camera clicked; my camera clicked. It was a long, long meet. The score went back and forth again and again, but I couldn't really bring myself to notice the sporting tension in the middle of all this personal agitation.

The last event of the night was a relay, and Linnie was the final swimmer for our team. Naturally, the winner would take all . . . but Angelika had told me not to shoot Linnie. This was killing me. All I could think about was Grampa saying, *Get the shot.* And those kids in the lunchroom saying, *You took that picture? Dude. I'm in awe.* Oh, yeah, and Linnie saying, *Make me look beautiful.* I glanced at my partner, who was quietly packing up her gear. She sighed and said, "Go on, Pete — shoot away. We wouldn't want our male readers to be disappointed, would we?"

Linnie won, but it felt like somehow I was losing.

After the meet, Angelika and I went upstairs through the deserted halls of the school. We needed to go to the newspaper office and download our picture files. Things were so tense I couldn't stand it, so I started saying stuff like "Hey, doesn't this remind you of one of those high school murder movies? Ooh . . . woo . . ." Which is (A) completely lame, and (B) completely not like me. But Angelika was as good at silence as my grandfather was — and that was about a thousand times better than I could handle.

She finally spoke, and her voice was all business: "Did you get anything good?"

As usual, her quick-transition trick left me struggling to switch gears. "Uh, I th-think so," I stammered. Once I got going, though, I could feel myself blabbering in a semi-panic. "I went over the check-list you made, and I got everyone we wanted. I mean, everyone we needed. I mean, I don't think we have to go to any more swim meets if the shots, um, look good."

By this point, we were at the office. This part was a little more comfortable, because it was a routine; it was exactly the same every time we shot a sport-ing event. Angelika tapped on the space bar of the iMac we used for photo edits, and held out a hand for my memory card. I handed the card over, she slid it into a card reader, and we stood together and watched as the images popped up in neat rows on the monitor.

Angelika made technical comments about the pics: Some needed to be cropped, some were a bit too bright, and a few were a bit blurry. Still, though, as the photos flashed by, most looked pretty darn good, which meant that I had been right about not needing to go to another meet. That was welcome news, because I wasn't sure I'd survive being between Angelika and Linnie Vaughn again.

The last seven shots or so showed Linnie winning the relay: Her perfect dive. Her graceful stroke. Her amazingly slick flip-turn. The end of the race, when she stood on the deck and raised her glistening arms in victory. I barely even knew how to swim, but you didn't exactly have to be a dolphin to realize Linnie was something special in the water. Well, and out of it.

Of course, she was no Angelika. I almost got up my nerve and said something to that effect, but Angelika didn't give me enough time to get the words out. "You did great, Pete!" she practically hissed. "Your favorite subject is going to be so pleased. Maybe she'll even ask you to be her personal photographer. . . ."

I don't get mad very easily, but this was starting to irritate me. I mean, what had I done wrong? Angelika was the one who had volunteered me to be a sports photographer. All I did was show up at every single event she told me to, and take a bunch of pictures.

Excellent pictures, in fact, if I did say so myself.

Was it my fault that Linnie Vaughn looked good in a swimsuit?

I fished my spare memory card out of my pocket (with a silent thanks to my grandfather for drilling that tip into me), walked across the room to my camera bag, slapped the card into my camera, and got Angelika in the frame. She glared at me, one hand on her hip. "What are you doing, Peter?"

I started taking pictures.

"I'm serious," she said, stepping toward me. "What are you doing?"

I kept shooting.

"Come on, give me that," Angelika said.

Click, click, click. She was getting closer.

"No," I said.

"Why not?" she asked.

"Because Linnie freaking Vaughn isn't my favorite subject, Angelika. *You're* my favorite subject."

Through the viewfinder, I saw Angelika reach for my camera. I let her take it out of my hands, but the strap was still around my neck. She pulled the camera to her. I came along with it. I'm happy to say I didn't take any more pictures that night. But my girlfriend and I did make it to Linnie's party. Eventually.

"See, Pete here is the freaking luckiest guy there is," AJ declared. It was hours later, after Linnie's party had been broken up by the surprise arrival of her parents. AJ, Angelika, and I were sprawled out on the wicker furniture of the back porch of AJ's house. It was about forty degrees out, but I wasn't feeling the cold. There had been this delicious fruit punch at the party with watermelon in it, and — even though I swear I hadn't known it at the time — apparently some of the non-fruit ingredients weren't exactly legal for Pennsylvanians under the age of twenty-one. Linnie had taken a special interest in quenching our thirst for some reason, and the drink was so fruity and good that I might have picked up a refill or two before the festivities had met an aborted end. AJ had been a big punch fan, too.

Angelika had taken a sip, poured the rest of her drink into a potted plant, muttered, "Sorry, plant," and then proceeded to watch me and AJ ignore her warnings.

Anyway, now my head was in Angelika's lap, and my eyes were closed. She was playing with my hair, which felt really nice — so nice that I hadn't said a word in at least half an hour, because I was hypnotized by the sensation. She and AJ had both decided I was asleep, which meant the conversation was taking an interesting turn.

"Luckiest? What's so lucky about him?"

"Well, first of all he's got you massaging his scalp, while I'm sitting here all alone. I mean, not *alone* alone, but . . . you know. Alone."

"Oh," Angelika said, and I could hear the laugh in her voice. "So you're pretty much saying you're *alone*, then?"

"'S right. But Pete's got a girlfriend. You are his . . . I mean, he's your . . . you guys are all, like, girlfriend, boyfriend, boyfriend, girlfriend now, right?"

"Yeah," she said. "I think we are."

"'At's cool," AJ mumbled.

"So how else is he lucky?"

AJ snorted. "You kidding me? He's, like, Mr. Perfect Life. El Perfecto Grande. Captain Gots-it-all. Like, have you met his family? His mom is the awesomest mom there is. Did you know he, uh, sleepwalks sometimes?"

Dude, I thought. *Thanks a lot. I don't sleepwalk. I just wake up, and then walk. Angelika's going to think I'm some kind of zombie or something.*

Angelika must have shaken her head, because AJ continued. "And he goes to the kitchen table, right? So his mom wakes up — and this is, like, at *night* night. We're talking three in the morning. My mom would be all *What are you doing up, Adam James?* Uh, because that's my real name: Adam James. Anyway, she'd be going, *You should be in bed!* And I'd be thinking, *No duh, Mom!* And she'd go, *Here I am, a single mother, with you and your little brothers to worry about, plus a full-time job, and I don't have time for this, blah blah blah*, until I fell a-freaking-sleep just from hearing the same old stupid speech about why do I need any attention from her . . . uh, what was I talking about again?"

"Pete. Lucky."

"Oh, right. So his mom gets up, sits with him at the table, and feeds him cookies. I mean, not *feeds him* feeds him — she doesn't put them in his mouth or anything. But the point is, she's right there with the cookies and all. And then there's his dad. Pete complains because his dad works a million hours a week, but first of all, that's why Pete always gets everything he wants. And his dad is nice and everything when he's around. And neemwhile . . . I mean, meanwhile, my dad lives like a thousand miles away, and you don't hear *me* complaining about it."

"Except now," Angelika said.

"Well, yeah. But you don't hear me complaining about it when I'm, like, *sober*." There was a long silence, and I may have started to doze off, but then AJ said, really loudly, "Plus, have you met Pete's grandfather? He's freaking awesome. And I mean, I know he's old, and Pete's all worried about him and everything — but both of my grandfathers are *dead*. I'm not trying to be mean or anything: I love Pete's grampa. Did you know he's come to, like, every baseball game we've had for the past three years straight? And he's taken pictures at all of them. And then he puts them up online so everybody's parents can order prints if they want. And for me, that's a big deal. It's not like my mom actually gets to most of my games, with TJ and CJ — those are my brothers — to take care of. And I'm pretty sure my dad wouldn't even know what I *look* like if Mom didn't keep sending him those pictures."

My head was spinning. I had always thought AJ had the perfect life. His mom always let him go wherever he wanted; he was so much bigger, stronger, and better-looking than I was; and he was just so *relaxed*. I couldn't believe AJ was jealous of the things I *had* when I spent my life wishing I could be who he *was*. Plus, there was one other thing he had going for him. I almost opened my eyes and sat up to point it out, but fortunately, Angelika had my back.

"What about his elbow problem?" she said. "Don't you think that's pretty unlucky? I mean, I never knew him when he was playing baseball, but he seems pretty crushed that now he can't." *Go, Angelika*, I thought. "Did you know he even *cried* about it in front of me?" *Stop, Angelika*, I thought.

AJ said, "Yeah, I know how bad the arm thing is. Did you know I was there when it happened? He was pitching, and I was the catcher. The look on his face right before he fell — it was horrible. Don't tell Pete this, but I even had a couple of nightmares about it. Still, even then, his parents were both there, and his grandfather came charging out on the field, too. If it had happened to me, the coaches would have had to send my parents a freaking telegram or something."

Another long silence followed, which gave me more time to think about how much I hadn't understood about my best friend. I wasn't sure whether I should just lie there and be furious at him for blabbing all this stuff to Angelika, or sit up and ask for a group hug.

Then he started talking again. "Plus, I know he's going to pitch again."

"I'm not so sure about that, Adam. When he talks about it, he —"

"I know he says he might not. But that's because he flips out about everything. Trust me, he'll be back. He *has* to."

"Why?"

"Because . . . swear you won't say anything? Because this sounds really wussy."

"Um, I swear."

"He thinks he needs baseball, but that's not true. Well, he needs it, but he doesn't *need* need it. Not the way I do. He's got everything else. He takes the fall off from pitching and ends up getting straight As, becoming a freaking yearbook editor as a freshman, and going out with you. But me, I need baseball. I *am* baseball. Listen: Peter can do anything in the world he wants to do. *Anything* anything. But me? I can throw a ball. That's pretty much it. And — I'm almost at the wussy part. I'm scared to try out for the team without him."

"Why? Pete always tells me how cool and confident you are on the field. And I saw you play basketball. I took pictures of you on the court — and you're so, I don't know, graceful. You make sports look so effortless."

"Thanks. You know what, Angelika? Pete always tells me how smart *you* are. And he's right. But anyway, I pitch better with Pete behind the plate. He's so good at calling pitches. Plus, I just feel like when he's back there, I'm going to hit his glove every time. I don't know why. It's like he's my security blanket or something. *That's* the wussy part."

"Yeah, I could tell."

I couldn't help it: I snorted. Angelika was just such a fast thinker. Fortunately, my arm was kind of in front of my mouth, so the snort sounded more like a snore.

"I can see why you're so attracted to him, Angelika," AJ said. "He makes such, um, sexy noises."

"Oh, shut up."

13. death by fruit

Sunday was a horror. At some point in the early morning hours, I had passed out in Angelika's lap. At some later point, I had been woken up by a rush of vomit in my throat, tried to roll over, and spun to the ground from the hammock that AJ had somehow managed to move me to. Sadly, AJ's porch hammock is suspended about three feet above a brick floor. Brick is cold, it's hard, and it has one other really negative quality: Liquids splatter when they hit it.

By the time AJ came out to check on me at 5:45 A.M. or so, I was huddled on the wicker couch again, wrapped in a fuzzy-lined tarp I had pulled off of his mom's barbecue grill, shivering, and bleeding from abrasions to my right palm and my left knee. Which of course meant that (A) my pants were ripped, and (B) I had gotten blood all over the lining of the tarp. Plus, the whole front of my shirt was flecked with dried barf, and my head hurt like somebody was dropping a rock on it every half second. From a great height.

And the taste in my mouth? You don't even want to know.

Of course, AJ was in a fabulous mood. "Get up, brother Pete!" he said. "Here, I brought you some OJ." This announcement caused me to gag all over again. "Oopsie," AJ said. "Come on, drink this up . . . nice and slow now. . . ."

I took a few of the slowest sips in the history of the planet and was trying to decide whether I'd ever again be capable of swallowing more than one drop of fluid at a time when AJ said, "Ooh, stand up! Hurry! You have to get into the bathroom — pronto!"

His raised voice pounded against my brain, making the whole porch seem to spin and pulsate as I jumped to my feet. "Whuh . . . why?" I asked, in the throes of an insane head rush.

"Two words: Mom. Angelika."

Holy cow! In my shameful state, I had completely forgotten about Angelika. "Angelika? What happened? Where is she? Is she OK?" I grabbed at the arm of the couch with one hand to steady myself.

"She's fine — *she's* not the one who tossed back three cups of that punch like it was, uh, punch. But she's upstairs getting dressed, and you definitely want to get in the shower before she sees you."

"Wait. She's here. Where did she sleep? And where, uh — where did *you* sleep?"

I had a deeply serious moment of panic, which lasted until AJ said, "Ange slept in my bed . . ."

Ange? I thought. *Ange?*

". . . and I slept out here with you. I just got up way early — dude, I was so, like, starving! So I went in and scrounged around for something I could eat without waking anybody up. Lucky for me there was a Pop-Tart and some leftover Chinese shrimp with lobster sauce. . . ."

I barely stopped myself from hurling yet again.

"Anyway, I think you need to hit the lav right now, while Ange and my mom aren't walking the halls yet.

I mean, if I'm not actually lighting the house on fire or something, Mom doesn't usually notice what I'm doing too much. But she's pretty sensitive to smells, and — well — you reek like death. Stale death."

It's pretty hard to stage a one-man commando raid on a suburban tract house when one can barely stand, but I made it to the bathroom unseen. AJ knocked really quietly, and told me he would dig up a toothbrush, painkillers, and some clothes while I took a shower. By the time I got all cleaned up and came out, there was a pile of supplies on the counter. I brushed my teeth, gargled about forty-three gallons of mouthwash, combed my hair with my fingers, and forced myself to swallow a few Advils. Getting anything to go down my throat was a gruesome task, but on the other hand, I felt like someone was trying to squeeze my brain through a cheese grater — and that had to stop.

I surveyed the clothes AJ had left me: a pair of fluorescent orange sweatpants, boxer briefs, socks, and a bright red Phillies T-shirt. What a freaking crack-up that guy was. Even in his hungover state (although admittedly, he appeared to be handling the condition a million times better than I was), he had thought to make me — a die-hard Yankees fan — wear a Phillies garment. Angelika called my name and knocked on the door. I looked at the Phillies shirt. I sighed, said, "Hang on, I'm getting dressed," then blushed furiously as I reached for the mound of clothing.

Well, one thing I could say for this getup: The socks fit. Aside from that, I looked like some kind of gangsta sock puppet. Between the garish color scheme and the fact that AJ is nearly a foot taller and forty pounds heavier than me, I was not going to be featured in any fashion shows wearing this ensemble. Angelika knocked again. I started to open the door, but then realized my disgustingly filthy clothes were sitting in a pile on the floor. Thinking fast, I grabbed them up, dumped out the little bathroom garbage can onto the floor, took out the plastic trash bag inside it, scooped the garbage back up from the floor into the can, and tied the clothes inside the bag.

Whew, I thought, *that was a close one*. I took a deep breath, and opened the door. "Good morni —" was all I got out before Angelika stormed into the room, slamming the door shut behind her. She was wearing a pair of AJ's sweats, too, but the look was a whole lot cuter on her.

"NEVER do that to me again!" she growled, stamping her foot.

"What did I do?"

"You put me in a bad situation, Peter! You passed out, and left me in a strange house, with no way to get home."

"It's not a strange house. It's AJ's house, and he's —"

"Shut. Up. I only want to say this once: If you ever, ever get drunk when you are supposed to be my date, you will never be my date again. Got it?"

That Advil simply was not going to be strong enough to take away all the pain I was having. Rubbing my temples with one hand, I nodded. "Good," Angelika said. "Now. Are you OK, Peter?" The next thing I knew, she was hugging me. That's the bad thing about dating somebody who thinks faster than you do: You never quite know what the heck is going on.

A pounding on the door made us jump apart. It also made me grab the side of my head again. Angelika touched my cheek gently, then spun and turned the knob. This time, AJ's mother stormed in. She looked at Angelika, said, "Out!" and then wheeled on me. Angelika tiptoed past her, left the room, and closed the door softly. This was just what I needed: another angry confrontation. I didn't get it. AJ's mom had always been completely uninvolved. There had been dozens of nights when I had slept over without even seeing her in the morning. We'd come downstairs, and she'd already be gone out to do errands with AJ's brothers or something. The closest I got to contact with her on most of those mornings was the note she'd leave on the counter:

Boys —
Make your beds. There's coffee made,
and the Hostess donuts are somewhat
fresh. Be good —

                                        M.

So why, on this of all mornings, was she all agitated?

"Peter Friedman," she said. "I am *so* mad at you. I trusted you. I always trust you. You are supposed to be AJ's smart friend. I have never felt I had to worry when AJ was with you. Do you know what it's like to be a single mother, Peter? No, of course you don't. You can't. So I'll tell you: Being a single mother means not having enough time. Not being able to take care of everything you need to take care of. And worrying. All. The. Time. But you've always been so levelheaded and responsible that I've felt good about leaving AJ alone with you."

She left off for a moment with that thought, and paced back and forth several times. I felt like I was locked in the bathroom with an enraged mama bear. "Um, Mrs. Moore, I'm really sorry I —"

"You think you're sorry? You stay out till all hours of the night, you bring my son home drunk, and then in the morning I find some strange GIRL in his bed?"

"Wait, she's not a strange girl, she's —"

"She's who? This ought to be good."

"She's my girlfriend. Angelika."

"Your girlfriend? In AJ's bed?"

I nodded and gulped. When she put it that way, it sounded kind of upsetting.

Mrs. Moore put her palm on the side of my head, and gave me a sort of half shove, half smack. "That's for AJ."

I stood there, trying not to sway.

She gave me another half smack. "That's for Angelika."

I was swaying. I was definitely swaying. I strongly hoped AJ's mom was done with forcibly moving my head for a while. She wasn't. She stepped close one more time, put her palms on both sides of my face, and shook me a few times. I thought my eyeballs were going to pop out onto her fuzzy bedroom slippers.

"That's for you," she said, and stomped out of the bathroom.

As you might imagine, breakfast was a little

awkward, although Angelika and Mrs. Moore got along like long-lost sisters. AJ's brothers chatted up a storm, too, while AJ sat there and didn't say much. Meanwhile, I was engaged in a desperate battle against the forces of nausea. AJ had told his mom that we had gotten drunk on fruit punch, so she had gotten some special revenge by preparing this meal:

- Apple pancakes with strawberry sauce
- Strawberry-banana-kiwi juice
- Orange yogurt
- Grapefruit
- Wildberry Toaster Strudel
- Froot Loops

But somehow I survived long enough to stagger out of there and walk Angelika home. Then I hiked my way back to AJ's house to pick up my putrid bag of laundry. When I got there, AJ was the only one still home. All I wanted to do was lie down on the couch and take a three-hour nap, but sadly, AJ had other plans. As soon as I walked in, he threw my old catcher's mitt at me and said, "Guess what. It's spring training time!"

Where had he even gotten that thing? Wherever it had come from, it hurt. I groaned, and said, "What are you talking about? It's November."

"Yeah, but you're out of shape. You didn't play soccer or basketball this year, and it shows. Look at you! You're all fat and soft. If we don't start working on you now, you're going to look like a marshmallow in your uniform by the time tryouts roll around."

"But —"

"No buts, Pete. Do you want Ange to dump you for someone who can run across the street *without* doubling over and gasping for air? Someone who doesn't suffer from the dreaded affliction known as muffin-top-itis?"

"Dude, I'm not —"

He patted me on the stomach, harder than strictly necessary, and said, "Yes. You are. You *so* are. Look at this jelly roll. Now let's go."

Muffin top? Jelly roll? AJ was nuts. On the other hand, I had nearly died of a heart attack running to Grampa's house. "Fine," I said. "Bring it. I'll show you who's in shape."

He was beaming now. "That's my boy," he said. "Finally showing some competitive fire. Now get your glove on and get out there so I can pitch to you."

"Uh, AJ, I'm still not allowed to throw."

"I know, I know. The physical therapist has you on a special program, right?"

I nodded. What I didn't tell him was that the program consisted of me relearning how to do extremely basic low-impact movements. Like tying my shoe, for example.

"So, no worries. You won't throw today." He grabbed the glove out of my hand. "You'll run!"

But first, I had to start a load of laundry. For the record, I would just like to point out that I didn't throw up while I was putting my clothing in the washer. It was touch and go there for a while, especially when I had to peel the folds of my shirt apart where they had been glued together by whatever goop I had brought forth from the depths of my stomach, but I held on to my revolting fruity breakfast.

I would also like to point out that I didn't vomit during the two-mile run that AJ subjected me to. I felt like my head was going to burst open like a rotting, gas-filled pumpkin, and every step made my guts lurch and roll, but again, there was no display of liquefied Froot Loops. Even after the run, when AJ said, "So much for the warm-ups. Now it's sprinting time!" I held it all together through several rounds of suicide drills on the school's outdoor basketball courts.

But when we got back to AJ's house, his mother was home. As soon as we walked in, she smiled wickedly at me and said, "Oh, good! You're up and about! That's the way to handle your first hangover. I'm proud of your fortitude." I smiled back at her, but I'd imagine it was a weak and sickly little grin. Then she hustled into the kitchen and came back holding a huge tumbler full of garish hot-pink fluid.

Thick, garish hot-pink fluid. "I've made you a little post-workout treat, Peter. How would you like a nice glass of watermelon smoothie?"

I managed to get half of that sucker down. *Then* I threw up.

14. catch 'em lookin' good

By the time Monday rolled around, my head and stomach had mostly settled back into feeling like parts of my body. My legs were extraordinarily tight and sore, but other than that, I was ready to get back to school. I was even eager to get to photography class to see Angelika.

I walked in and found a quote written on the board:

WE PHOTOGRAPHERS DEAL IN THINGS WHICH ARE CONTINUALLY VANISHING, AND WHEN THEY HAVE VANISHED THERE IS NO CONTRIVANCE ON EARTH WHICH CAN MAKE THEM COME BACK AGAIN. WE CANNOT DEVELOP AND PRINT A MEMORY. ~HCB

I sat down, and Ange came in right behind me. Ange? Ugh. Now I was calling her that. Anyway, I wasn't sure if she would still be mad from my weekend escapades, but she smiled and said, "Feeling better today?" I smiled back and nodded. "Did you go running with Adam?" I nodded, but thought, *How does she know that?* I wasn't sure it was a good idea to have Angelika getting all palsy-walsy with AJ.

Mr. Marsh strode in and said, "Hey, guys, happy Monday! Now, we got lots ta do today. I wanna check out yer candids, or at least the ones ya got so far."

Several people walked up to the board and pinned up their photos. Mr. Marsh walked down the line of prints, saying, "Crap, crap, ka-rapppp! ka-rappp! crap, decent, decent, crap, ka-rappp!"

Danny, the senior dude, muttered, "Tell us how you *really* feel, Mr. Marsh."

"Danny, did you take these three photos in the middle?" Mr. Marsh tapped on a trio of close-up shots of a bunch of cheerleaders hanging all over each other in front of some lockers.

Danny nodded. "Yeah, I did. So? They're all in focus, right? And even though the light in the senior hallway is horrible, the exposure looks good, too. Doesn't it? Plus, look at the composition. See how the girls' faces make a pyramid? I thought that had great visual irony. 'Cause they're cheerleaders, right? And it's a pyramid. So . . ."

"So," Mr. Marsh said, icily, "you ignored the stated assignment completely. These aren't candid shots. They're the most posed pictures I've ever seen!"

"Yeah, but —"

"Danny, in twenty-five years, is this how these girls will want to remember their time at this school?"

"Sure. Why not? They were *loving* the camera. *They* were the ones who were getting all excited about posing. Plus, in twenty-five years, they'll probably be, like, all sagged out and old, right? So they'll go to their yearbook, and they'll show their daughters these shots. And they'll say, 'See? I was a complete *babe* when I was your age!'"

"I see. And is this how their fellow students will want to remember them?"

"Uh, I know this is how *I'll* want to remember them."

"San," Mr. Marsh said, "what was it you said the other day about the goal of candid photography?"

San had been in his usual near-comatose state of relaxation, leaning all the way back in his chair with his feet perched on his desk. He suddenly sat up straight so that the front legs of his chair slammed to the floor with a sharp *Spanggg!* "Truth, Mr. Marsh." He put his feet back up, rearranged his hands behind his head, and within three seconds, he was totally still again.

"Truth!" Mr. Marsh said. "These shots might be in focus, Danny. They might have textbook-perfect exposure. They might be well-composed. But they're not the truth. They're, like, the *High School Musical* version of the truth. And I am not tryin' ta produce the Walt Disney High School yearbook."

Erika, who probably felt like she should stand up for her fellow senior, chimed in: "So what are you telling us? Are you saying we're not supposed to make people look *good* in their own yearbook?"

"Of course ya want 'em ta look good, Erika. But Henri Cartier-Bresson would tell you it isn't yer job ta *make* 'em look good. It's yer job ta *catch* 'em lookin' good! That way, they have the moment forever. In fact, ya know what? That's yer new assignment, guys: Find somebody — anybody — and catch 'em lookin' good."

After school that day, Angelika and I were hanging out on the steps. Her mom was going to pick her up a little late, so I decided to keep her company. She was kind of pumped up with Mr. Marsh's new idea: Catch 'Em Lookin' Good! "Pete, this is perfect! Your grampa used to take pictures of all your games, right?"

"Yeah, why?"

"Because this year, obviously, he won't be shooting the baseball games."

"And that's perfect how?"

"Well, somebody has to shoot those games so Adam has pictures to send to his dad. In fact, that's going to be my project. I'll make a portfolio of Adam in action."

"Why AJ? Why not me?"

"You know why it won't be you."

"What are you talking about?"

She looked away from me and said, "Pete, I *know*."

Have you ever gotten that sudden heart-lurching feeling, like your heart just stopped and it's not going to beat again? That's what happened to me at that instant. "What are you talking about?"

"I know you're not going to be playing baseball, OK? My dad is an X-ray technician. I told him about your osteochondritis dissecans thing, and he asked around."

"Uh, well, I —"

"Don't lie to me, Peter. I forgave the drinking thing — once — but I don't do lying."

I didn't say anything for what felt like minutes. When neither of us could take another instant of silence, she said, "It's true, right? You can't play baseball anymore?"

I nodded. She said, "I'm so sorry, Pete. And I'm not mad at you for not telling me. But why haven't you fessed up to AJ?"

"I've tried to tell him. Like ten times. He doesn't listen. I say, 'I don't think I'm going out for the team,' and he just goes, 'Yes, you are, dude!'"

"But you haven't just told him the facts, straight out. I know you haven't. He talked to me about it the other night when you were, um, sleeping."

"This isn't about AJ. It's about me."

"So your best friend doesn't deserve to know what's going on?"

I felt a flash of anger. "It's not AJ's problem, is it?"

"What are you talking about?" she said.

"AJ's not the one who screwed up, is he? AJ's not the one who knew he was wrecking his arm, but didn't freaking tell anyone for a whole season. AJ's the one who can throw eighty miles an hour all day without even sweating, so AJ never had to worry about trying to throw harder and harder until his elbow exploded. And now AJ's going to be the stud pitcher as a freshman. So I don't see how it's AJ's freaking problem that he'll be getting his picture taken by my girlfriend while I'm sitting in the stands alone eating a stupid hot dog!"

Oopsie. That might have come out a tad more forcefully than I'd meant it to. Angelika didn't seem pleased. "Well, maybe it won't be that way," she said.

"What do you mean? I just admitted I'm not going to be playing, OK?"

"No, that's not what I mean. Maybe your *girlfriend* won't be taking pictures of AJ. Because if you don't trust people with your secrets, and if you get this jealous all the time, maybe I won't *be* your girlfriend!"

Ouch. "Wait, I wasn't trying to yell at you, OK? It's just — this year has been really horrendous for me."

She raised an eyebrow. I barreled on. "I had this whole fantasy. AJ and I were going to be the big star pitchers of the school. And instead he's going to be the star, and I'm crippled. Meanwhile, my grandfather is losing his freaking mind, and my parents don't believe it. Plus, he's telling me to lie to cover up for him."

Angelika looked like I had just slapped her or

something. "Ooh, you're right, Pete. This *has* been a terrible year for you. I'm sorry your life sucks so much! Gee, if only you had *met somebody special* this year, or something . . ."

I had put my foot in my mouth again. Great. If I kept this up, pretty soon I'd be the only guy I knew with a case of Athlete's Tooth. Just then, with the perfect timing that I enjoy in so many aspects of my existence, Angelika's mom pulled up. "Uh . . ." I said.

"Bye, Pete."

"Wait!" I shouted. Angelika's mom looked nervously at me, at her daughter's red face, and then back at me. "Can't we talk?"

"Gotta go," Angelika said. "Why don't you tell AJ the truth? *Then* we can talk."

Sitting alone on the front steps of school is embarrassing enough when you haven't just been left in the dust by a girl. But this was mortifying. So of course everyone I knew was staying late that day and happened to walk by while I was deciding what to do next. It was a veritable flood: AJ, surrounded by a group of his basketball friends. Danny from photography. My homeroom teacher. My biology lab partner, Matt. Then, finally, when it seemed like the entire building had to be empty, San Lee.

Everybody else accepted my weak little half-wave maneuver and kept walking, but San actually sat down next to me. It was kind of weird. He and I had never really spoken — in fact, as far as I knew, he rarely spoke much at all. Yet, here we were: a very tense freshman and a junior who looked like he might fall asleep any second. "Hey," San said, stretching his legs out in front of him so he was leaning back on his elbows. "What's going on?"

"Nothing."

He raised one eyebrow. It's amazing how many people do that to me. "Really?" he said. "Because you look pretty bummed."

"I'm fine. Really."

There went that eyebrow again.

"Look, thanks for asking. But I don't want to talk about it."

"Did you have a fight with Angelika?"

I forced myself to laugh. "Angelika? Angelika who? Oh, you mean that girl in photography?"

The brow shot up even higher. *Watch out, San*, I thought. *If somebody hits you on the back right now, you could be stuck that way for life.* At least that was what my mom had always told me whenever I started crossing my eyes at dinner to make Samantha laugh.

"Yeah, that girl in photography. The one who's been your partner all year. Come on, like you don't know you're the pet freshman couple of the class?"

I sighed. "Yeah, I had a fight with Angelika. What do you care, anyway? And why are you even around this late?"

"I'm around this late because my girlfriend is inside practicing for the talent show. And I care because — well, what the heck? I'm sitting here anyway. I might as well be trying to help somebody."

"Uh, thanks. I guess. But there's nothing anybody can do to solve the problem right now. You have any advice for how to stop feeling like I just got chewed up and spit out?"

He closed his eyes and thought about that one for a while. Then, all of a sudden, a shadow fell on us. I looked up, and a girl was standing there, holding a banged-up guitar case and smiling down at San. She was pretty, in a frizzy-headed semi-hippie-ish kind of way. She kicked his foot, and he said, "Hey, Emily." Then he stood up and they kissed for so long I was embarrassed to be sitting there.

When the epic lip-lock finally broke, Emily said, "What's up, San?"

He gestured down at me. "My freshman companion here has a problem. He wants to know what to do when you feel totally bummed about a problem you can't solve."

"Hi, freshman companion — uh, what's your name?"

"Pete," I said.

"Hi, Pete. You know, San and I have both been in this situation, and do you know what we did?"

I just looked at her blankly. How was I supposed to know what they had done? I barely even knew him, and all I knew about her was that she had big hair, and kissed with great fervor.

"We both did the exact same thing, and it totally worked."

"Oh, yeah? What was it?"

"We found somebody who needed help, and then we helped them. It sounds corny, but once you start helping people, your own stuff just kind of . . . well . . . falls into place. Come on, San."

He bent his knees and kind of crouched down so his eyes were just above the level of mine. "You going to be all right?"

"I, uh, I guess so. I think I'll be going now, before anybody else stops by to give me unsolicited couples therapy." He stood and started to walk away, hand in hand with Emily.

I felt bad as soon as the words had come out of my mouth. This was the second time in an hour I had snapped at somebody who tried to give me advice. "Wait," I said. They both turned. "Thanks," I said. "But who am I supposed to help?"

"Who needs it the most?" San asked. Then he and Emily strolled across the front walkway of the school, and got into the last car in the student parking lot.

15. No Contrivance on earth

For the next few weeks, things were tense with Angelika. It was pretty darn annoying, because she kept texting AJ about me ("Pete has something to tell you!"), and texting me about AJ ("Told him yet?"). Then AJ would text me about Angelika, and text her about me. He was in this odd kind of Dr. Phil role, and believe me: AJ might be my best friend, but that doesn't qualify him to be a relationship counselor.

Here's a typical session between AJ and me, from the day before Thanksgiving:

AJ: So, what's the deal? Are you guys, like, back together yet? Because truthfully, this is getting kind of stressful for me.
Me: Stressful for you? I'm the one who had a

girlfriend for two and a half days, followed by a month of nonstop tension.

AJ: Actually, marriage counseling happens to be one of the most stressful professions.

Me: And you know this how?

AJ: It's just known. Why are you always asking me how I know stuff? If you say the sky is blue, I don't ask you for a freaking bibliography of sources to prove it.

Me: Sigh.

AJ: Anyway, you're only being all snippy with me because you're displaying classic resistance.

Me: Resistance? What are you talking about?

AJ: It's when a patient's unconscious mind works to undermine the relationship between the patient and the therapist. Don't worry, it's quite common. Plus, it prob'ly means you're on the verge of a major breakthrough.

Me: And you know this how?

AJ: Haven't you ever watched that psychologist reality show on cable? You know — *The Nut Boss?*

Me: Um, I must'a missed that one, but whatever. Listen: Can't you just give me, like, normal boy-girl advice?

AJ: Sure. Buy her some freaking daisies.

Me: Daisies? That's all you've got?

AJ: Or roses. Chicks totally dig roses.

Me: Thank you, Dr. Freud.

On Thanksgiving, my family has a tradition: My grandfather comes over in the morning, and we watch the Phillipsburg–Easton high school football game. They're these two towns about half an hour from where we live, and they've been huge football rivals for something like 107 years. My dad went to Phillipsburg High, and Grampa went to Easton, so it's a pretty big deal in our house. I know this sounds totally sexist — but Samantha helps Mom in the kitchen all morning while the three genera-tions of men sit in front of the TV and argue about the game.

But this year was different. This year, Grampa couldn't keep up his end of the conversation. I don't think Dad noticed — give Dad a beer, chips, and a wide-screen TV, and he wouldn't notice if Godzilla sat down next to him on the couch. But I couldn't stand it. Dad would complain about a call, which in previous years would have made Grampa snort in disgust. This year, Grampa just grunted. Dad would jump up and cheer when his team scored, which always used to make Grampa say, "Oh, sit down, there's a lot of game left." This year, Grampa just looked kind of baffled. So I sat there and fumed, wondering how on God's green earth these people could possibly be oblivious to what was so clear to me.

When halftime finally came, after what felt like a million years, I had to get out of that room for a while. I asked Grampa if he wanted to come down and see what I was working on in photo class. Of course, he came, but looking at pictures didn't immediately snap him out of his fog like I had hoped it would. I showed him my portraits of Angelika, which he had already seen, but still, I liked looking at them. "Pretty girl," he said. I started to smile; he might not have remembered the pictures, but at least he thought my semi-girlfriend was attractive. "Who took these?" he continued. I reminded him that we were looking at my work, and he grinned, but kind of vaguely.

Next, I clicked through some of the best sports shots I had taken, and for some reason, he seemed more focused on these. Looking at one particularly tack-sharp photo I had taken of AJ going up for a rebound in basketball, he even asked me what lens I had used. I told him it was his old favorite 85mm prime lens, and he got all excited. "I love that lens," he said. "Can I see it?"

I was a bit taken aback, because he hadn't wanted to get involved with the actual equipment of photography for months. I went and got the lens out of my camera bag, though. He took it in his hands and turned it over and over, bending his neck and squinting intently. "That's not my lens. What camera would take a strange-looking piece of glass like that?" he spat.

I took it back from him, set it down on the computer desk, and scrambled to get his best Nikon camera body. Then I attached the lens, and held it out to him. "This is the camera, Grampa," I said quietly. "It's your best body. You always called it 'Numero Uno.'"

He laughed. "Numero Uno? That thing? That's not Numero Uno — it's not even one of my cameras. First of all, Numero Uno is a Leica. Second of all, Numero Uno isn't nearly that big. Or that fancy-looking. All those buttons and dials — I wouldn't even know where to put in the film!"

"Uh, it doesn't take film."

"What are you talking about? A camera that doesn't take film! What does it print onto — toilet paper?"

"Gramp," I said as gently as I could, "it's a digital camera. It saves all its images onto a memory card." I held the camera out for him to examine more closely.

He looked and looked at that camera, then sat down heavily in the chair, looking absolutely defeated. "I'm losing it, Peter. Don't tell your mother, but I am losing it."

I didn't know what to say. Really, who would?

I stood over him for a while, still holding the camera out like a moron. Then he said, "The other day, I forgot your grandmother's name for a minute. We were married for fifty years, and I forgot her name. What am I going to do? I don't want to forget my own wife."

I didn't want my grandfather to know I had noticed the tears that were trickling down his face, so I pretended to be scrutinizing the camera. I even mumbled the button functions to myself: "Aperture. Flash. ISO. Video Record."

Video record! I thought of San saying, "Who needs it the most?" I thought of Henri Cartier-Bresson's words: "We cannot develop and print a memory." But maybe I could, in a way. Maybe I could help my grandfather record what he remembered before it was gone forever. I ran and got Grampa a tissue, then attached the camera to a tripod while he dried his eyes.

I focused the camera right on Grampa's face, and said, "Hey, Gramp. Can you tell me how you and Grandma met?" Then I pressed the VIDEO RECORD button.

"It was the first day of classes at New York University, 1958. My first class, Portrait Photography, had just ended, and I'd sprinted the three blocks to my next class. I got to the lecture hall early, carrying my huge Psychology 101 textbook in one hand, and my camera in the other. I sat down in the third row, because you should never sit in the first two rows. It makes you look like a kiss —

"Um, wait . . . what were we talking about again? Oh, right, your grandmother. She walked in and my heart stopped. She was wearing a bright green dress. I dropped my book, and it made a loud BANG! on the tile classroom floor. I grabbed Numero Uno, and swung it up just as she looked to see where the noise had come from. If not for that Leica camera, who knows what would have happened. I got the shot, I got the girl . . . and I got a C-minus in psych! With your grandmother next to me, who could concentrate?"

● ● ● ● ● ● ● ● ●

By the time we got called back upstairs for dinner, Grampa was pretty cheerful. I didn't know whether recording his memories would slow down whatever was happening to his brain, but it had definitely helped his mood. I felt good, too, like I was finally doing something besides sitting around and worrying. Plus, Grampa had looked so vibrant and alive when he talked about my grandmother — and there was so much I hadn't known! I mean, I had seen the black-and-white photo of a very young Grandma in a dress on Grampa's dresser a million times, but I hadn't known he'd taken it in the first minute of their life together.

As soon as we had all piled our plates high with food, my dad announced that we were going to do the dreaded say-what-you're-thankful-for thing before we ate. Samantha rolled her eyes, but when it was her turn she said, "I have a lot to be thankful for this year. I'm so thankful that we could all be here together today. I'm thankful that I was lucky enough to be born into a family that could afford to pay for my college. And my car. Especially in this economy, with gas being so expensive and all. Of course, I almost have enough in my account to keep up, as long as I don't try to spend too much on fun things, or go to any parties, or —"

Dad cleared his throat.

"Anyway, I'm thankful for David —"

(That's her boyfriend at college. She hadn't managed to say three sentences without mentioning him in the two days she'd been home.)

"I'm thankful for Mom and Dad, for Grampy —"

(Yes, she actually called him Grampy.)

"And for my little brother, who is apparently taking over the high school. As a freshman! Impressive! Now, when do I get to meet this Angelina chick? I can't believe Petey is old enough to have a girlfriend!"

"Uh, it's Angelika. And she's not exactly my —"

Mom cut me off. "Can we get back to being thankful? We have the rest of the year to bicker, OK? Peter, would you like to go next?"

"I guess so." I took a deep breath, and tried to organize my thoughts. There was some irritating stuff happening in my life, and some truly bad stuff. But I thought about the things AJ had said about my life when he'd thought I was asleep, and it hit me that there was a lot of good stuff, too.

"I'm thankful for Grampa, for the time I get to spend with him, and for everything he's taught me about photography. Well, about everything, really. And for all the amazing equipment. I'm thankful to Mom, for making me take photography class this year. I'm thankful that I have good friends who care about me. And a family. And, um, that's it. So, thanks."

Smooth, I know. Somehow, my family managed to hold their applause. Mom reached over and squeezed my hand, though. "Next?" she said.

My dad, who had been fiddling with one of the wings from the turkey because it kept dripping grease onto the tablecloth, stopped what he was doing and started to make a big old speech. It kind of figured that he wouldn't say more than seventeen words the whole rest of the year, but then, when we were sitting in front of our first home-cooked meal in months, watching the sauces cool and congeal by the second, he'd suddenly start speechifying. But if he didn't hurry, I was afraid the mashed potatoes would harden into a thick mass of fork-destroying glop.

"We are lucky today to be in the presence of our loved ones, who have traveled great distances to join together and break bread . . ."

("Traveled great distances?" Samantha's college was maybe eighty-five miles away. And "break bread"? Who says "break bread"? Honestly, Dad.)

I played with my cranberry sauce, trying to see whether I could free a berry from the Jell-O-y part and leave a berry-shaped indentation. That's harder than you might think, so I missed most of Dad's oration. I tuned back in right at the end, when he said, ". . . and I am most thankful that I have a good job so I can work as hard as I have to, and make ends meet when, uh, additional expenses arise. Crises come and crises go, but I am very fortunate that so far, we have gotten through all of our crises . . . together."

(I wasn't sure what the additional expenses were, aside from the demands of Samantha's party budget, but I had certainly noticed the extra work Dad had been putting in. I didn't stop to wonder for too long, though, because then it was Grampa's turn.)

Grampa didn't say anything for the longest time. I noticed his eyes were wet and red-rimmed again, and I was pretty sure his hands were shaking. *This isn't you, Grampa*, I thought. *You don't shake. You don't cry.* "I'm thankful," he said, then stopped. He cleared his throat and started over: "I'm thankful for the girl in the green dress." Then, right there at the table, he broke down and sobbed.

16. well, that's one discussion over with

I texted Angelika that night:

Happy T-G! Cn I come ovr?

She wrote back in thirty seconds, tops:

Y?

Grampa probs. Need 2 talk.

Need 2 talk 2. Happy T-G! Get here @ 9?

I got there at nine. Angelika's mom let me in. Angelika was curled up on her living room couch in sweats, holding a ginormous mug of what turned out to be hot chocolate. Soon I was sitting stiffly at the far end of the couch with a huge mug of my own. Angelika's dad was nowhere to be found, but Angelika's mom sat down on a big easy chair about four feet away from me and started chatting her head off. Clearly, she was determined to be her daughter's chaperone for the evening.

All I wanted to do was talk to Angelika about my grandfather, and ask what problems she was having. But it was kind of hard, because her mom was hovering like a bathrobe-clad she-hawk, firing off question after question: How's school? How's the newspaper? How's the yearbook? How's your friend AJ? — I haven't seen him around for days!

(*Hoo boy*, I thought. *AJ's been around?*)

I tried to be as boring as possible with my answers, hoping I could just wear her out until she gave up, decided I was too slow-witted to be any threat to her daughter, and fled upstairs. It didn't work. Whenever her mom looked away, though, Angelika rolled her eyes and made apologetic faces — which at least let me know she wanted to be alone with me, too.

This weird stalemate was only broken when Angelika's dad called for her mom to come upstairs. As soon as she did — after one last, lingering look at her daughter — Angelika stretched her legs out so her feet were just touching the side of my left leg. "Hey," she said. I didn't know what the heck was going on with our so-called relationship, but one thing was for sure: All Angelika had to do to make me fall completely in testosterone with her again was give me two feet and a "hey."

"Uh, hi," I mumbled.

"So what's the problem?" she asked. "Lumpy potatoes? Dry turkey? Too much of the dreaded green-bean-and-cream-o'-mushroom casserole?"

I tried hard to forget about her feet against my leg — which was tough, because every once in a while, just when I was almost ready to stop sweating, she would wiggle her toes. I tried even harder to forget about the weirdness we'd been going through. I tried hardest of all to block out my questions about why *AJ had been coming to her house.* And I told her all the latest news about my grandfather. She listened silently, through several rounds of toe wiggling and a few sneak peaks through the stair railing by her mother.

When I had wound up my sad little monologue, I said, "Angelika, how much time did you have before your grandmother . . . you know . . . uh?"

She pulled her feet away from me and curled her arms around her knees. Suddenly, I could breathe. "What do you mean?"

"I mean, how long was it between when you first knew something was wrong and when she totally couldn't function anymore?"

Angelika said, "So I'm guessing you haven't told your parents about your grandfather's blanking-out episodes yet? I'm sure it's not the same for everybody, but I don't think you have a huge amount of time. I think with Grandma, from the first time we noticed anything major to the time she needed to be put in a home was only maybe six months. But you know, Pete —"

"I know. I should tell my mom everything."

"That wasn't what I was going to say . . . even

though you *know* I was thinking it. I was going to say, if you need any help with the video, I'll be glad to come along."

"Thanks. I'm going over to his house tomorrow to do some more filming. Maybe I'll ask him if it would be all right. I mean, I'd really like to have you there."

Angelika stretched so that her feet were against me again. "OK," she said. "Now I have a question for you. What kind of girls does Adam like?"

I moved away from her. Of all the questions in the world, this had to be up there with the all-time, world-record-breaking mood killers. I was tempted to say something that would reflect really badly on AJ. But then again, he was my best friend. I would just have to be as noble as I could in this horrible situation. "Well," I said, "he's — um — well, I don't think he likes one specific type of girl."

Translation: He's so hormone-crazed that if you're breathing, you're his type.

"OK, I'll break this down. Does he like short girls?"

Yeah, like I couldn't freaking see where this was heading. But I nodded. "Sure," I said. Because, you know, short girls generally *do* breathe.

"How about dark-haired girls?"

Crap. I nodded again, and edged all the way over against the far arm of the couch.

"With glasses?"

Good God, why didn't she just rip out my heart and stomp on it? I used every ounce of my willpower to wrestle my mouth into a grin. "Glasses are fine," I said. "I'm telling you, AJ just isn't that picky. OK?" I tensed my legs and got ready to walk out of there with some shred of dignity intact.

"Wow, this is perfect!" Angelika exclaimed.

I didn't see what kind of perfect this was, other than perfectly screwed-up. I stood and grabbed my cocoa mug.

Angelika jumped to her feet, and said, "Elena is going to be so happy!"

I put down the mug and whirled to face her. "Elena? Elena who?"

"Elena Zubritskaya!"

"Elena Zubritskaya?"

"You know, the Russian girl with the really big, um . . ."

"Accent?"

"Yeah, her. See, I've been working on my photos of Adam — you know, for the project? Catch 'em lookin' good?"

"Yeah, and?"

"Well, I was carrying a big blowup poster I made of Adam blocking a shot in basketball, and she asked what I was carrying. When I showed her, she said, 'I always think he so cute!' So I figured maybe . . . well, Adam just seems so lonely sometimes, so I thought maybe the two of them could . . . I don't know . . . get together. What do you think?"

Now my smile was genuine. Also huge. "I think it's genius! Because, truthfully, I had kind of thought that you and Adam — AJ — Adam . . . I kind of thought you and he, um, had something."

She laughed. "Me and Adam? Are you kidding?"

"Well, he's this big sports stud, and he's so much fun to be around. And I'm, like, Mister Depression.

Plus, you sleep in his bed, and you're suddenly taking pictures of him. Then he's coming over to your house, and you're all mad at me for not telling him about my arm. So I just figured —"

She grabbed my hand and pulled me down so we were sitting on the couch together. Close together. "Pete," she said, "you're right. Adam is cute, in a big sheepdog kind of way. And he is really fun. But I like intense guys. Smart, intense guys. I like you."

"But . . ."

"Believe me, OK? Listen, I'll tell you why I like you. Remember the first time we met, when I caught you staring at me, so I made a joke about it — and you blushed? And then you laughed and got busted by the teacher?"

"Um, I wasn't staring, I was . . . all right, I *was* staring. So?"

"So then I asked to switch classes, too. Because . . ."

"Because that teacher was a moron?"

"Well, yeah. But also because I wanted to get to know you. Not Adam. You!"

"Really?"

"Peter, I don't care who can throw a ball harder. You're the one that blushed when you looked at me. You're the one who's so concerned with your grandfather — guys never show that kind of emotion. You're different. And then — remember when I came over to do your portrait?"

"Of course."

"And do you remember how much I was flirting with you?"

"You were doing that on purpose?"

"Duh." *Wow,* I thought. *AJ was actually right about a girl. Who knew?* She continued, "So there I was, like, playing with my bra strap while you snapped away. But the one picture you chose out of the whole set was the one where I wasn't posing at all."

"The one with the brownies."

"The one with the brownies. It was like you're so sweet that you made *me* look sweet. Does that make any sense?"

"Nope," I said, and leaned toward her. When we kissed, I could feel that she was smiling.

● ● ● ● ● ● ● ● ● ● ●

Every day for the rest of the long Thanksgiving week-end, I did two things. First, I went running in the freezing cold with AJ. Next, I headed over to my grandfather's house with a camera and shot video. He really seemed to love talking about his life, and I found out a ton of stuff I had never known. Some examples:

- He had gone to Vietnam as a newspaper photographer, gotten shot down in helicopters twice, and won a journalism award for his coverage of a big battle called the Tet Offensive right before my mom was born. But he gave up his career as a combat photographer when my grandmother called him home. Or, as he put it, "She told me I could sleep in ditches and get shot at all day, or I could come home, sleep in our warm bed, and change diapers. It was a close call — some of your mother's diapers were pretty toxic — but the only thing in the world more important than your career is your family. Never forget that."

- He had shot the weddings of three future members of Congress, two famous rock musicians, one murderer, one reality-TV star, and all four children of a legendary race car driver. He had done weddings in chapels, in huge megachurches, in mosques, on the tops of mountains, on an airplane, in the middle of the ocean on a yacht, and even underwater with scuba gear. But his all-time favorite wedding was the very first legal gay marriage performed in Connecticut, between two middle-aged men. "Why?" I asked. He grinned. "It was the easiest shoot ever," he said. "No bride!"

- He and my grandmother had been married for half a century, and had only had three major arguments. The first was when he came home from Vietnam and found out she had gotten their house painted pink. "Your grandma Joanie told me it had looked like more of a brick red on the paint sample sheet," Grampa said. "A wonderful woman, but she had no sense of color."

The second argument was the day after my mom's high school graduation, when my grandmother had accidentally walked into his darkroom and ruined three rolls of film — every picture he had taken of Mom in her cap and gown. "That one was my fault," he said. "I didn't lock the door. I always, always locked the door. But my mother had cancer at the time, and it was getting pretty close to the end. I was so excited to get everything developed so I could rush over to the hospital and show her the photos of her granddaughter all grown up . . . eh, you know what? The reason doesn't matter. Whenever you're mad, there's always a reason. All that matters is, never yell at your wife. And you know what your great-grandmother said when I got to the hospital? I ran in there with a big bunch of flowers and told her the whole story. She said, 'I know how beautiful my own grandchild is. I don't need pictures for that.' Then she made me march right home and give Joanie the flowers."

The third argument had happened just a few weeks before my own grandmother's death from heart failure. Even four years after the fact, Grampa could barely talk about it. "I tried to get her out of bed. It was a beautiful day, and the docs kept saying the more she walked around, the better it would be for her heart. And we had always gone walking together. But she wouldn't get up. 'I'm tired,' she said. Over and over. But I wouldn't stop asking. Finally, she turned to me and said, 'I walked with you for half a century. Today, I can't do it. So would you please be quiet and just lie down next to me?'" Grampa started crying, and asked me to pause the recording for a minute. When he told me to start up again, he said, "Where was I? Oh, the last fight . . . you know what? Sometimes, letting go is the best you can do."

Grampa sat there for a while, nodding his head, lost in the memory. I stopped recording again, and waited without saying anything. For the first time

I could remember, Grampa was the one who broke the silence. "Do we have any tuna fish?" he asked.

I got up, ran into the kitchen, and checked. "Yes," I said. "We do."

"Um," he said, "do I like tuna fish?"

That was the bad part of spending so much time there: I had a close-up view of all the ways Grampa was slipping. He could remember the dress his dead wife had worn fifty-four years before, but in the present he wasn't sure whether he liked tuna. He could name maybe two thousand brides, but kept forgetting whether he had brushed his teeth that morning. And, because staring at someone through a zoom lens for an hour a day really makes you notice details, I saw that other things were starting to go: his collars were frayed. His sweaters were stained. His hair was a little clumpy. There were dust bunnies all over the house.

On Sunday afternoon, I asked him, "Grampa, are you all right?"

"What do you mean?"

"Well, I mean . . . are you doing OK living alone here?"

He sat back in his chair and closed his eyes for a while. Then he said, "It's hard, Peter. And it's getting harder. But I'm not ready to give up yet. All I want is to be the one that says *when*. All right?"

I nodded.

Suddenly, he leaned forward and clapped his hands together. "Well, that's one discussion over with," he said. "Now, do we still have any of that tuna?"

17. pitchers and catchers

Ah, December. The month of peace and candlelight. The month when all the good little children are lying snug in their beds, with visions of sugarplums dancing in their heads. The month when your best friend drags you to an unheated, godforsaken warehouse three times a week to practice for baseball tryouts.

Or maybe that last one just happens to me.

AJ's mom works for a lumber-distribution company, and every year since fifth grade or so, AJ and I have started our pitching/catching workouts in January in an empty corner of their massive storage facility right outside of town. This year, though, AJ was determined to start earlier than ever. He was obsessed with being in "*sick* he-man condition" in time for the indoor February junior varsity tryouts, and apparently, running me halfway to death was only the first part of the equation.

Thus, despite the constant warnings of my mother ("Do you *want* your arm to just fall off completely?") and my now-on-again girlfriend ("Do you *want* AJ to just punch you in the face and never talk to you again when he finds out the truth?"), I went with AJ. I kept meaning to tell him what was going on. But the moment had to be right, and the longer I waited, the harder it got. Plus, he really did need a practice catcher, and I wasn't hurting my bad arm just by warming him up. This might sound like an excuse, but the more time went on, the more I wanted AJ to make the team.

I wasn't totally stupid: I told him I wasn't ready to throw yet, so we brought a bucket of balls, and I just rolled each one off to the side after I caught it. Still, I could hardly believe that there I was, crouched down in catching position behind the home plate that AJ's dad had spray-painted onto the concrete floor back when he was still around. I was trying to field fastballs, breaking pitches, and my best friend's random thoughts all at once.

"Dude," he said, one morning between Christmas and New Year's, "was that a strike? By the way, thanks for the gift idea for Elena. When I gave it to her, she said, 'Is perfect!' How did you know she would get all happy about a book of love poems in Russian?"

"Angelika. She's like the Online Shopping Queen. She even got me this beastly Derek Jeter jersey for Hanukkah, when I never said anything to her about him."

Thwack! The next pitch exploded into my mitt, which really stings when it's only fifty freaking degrees in the room. "Uh, I gave her that idea," AJ said. "So, were the last *two* pitches strikes?"

"The first one was. The last one missed the corner."

Thwack! "How 'bout that one? And by the way, how do you expect to be ready in a month and a half if you won't even lob the ball back to me yet? Plus, do you think I need to update my style?"

"Um, strike, mind your own business, and why?"

Thwack! "Elena said I dress like a peasant."

"A peasant? She said that?"

Thwack! "Well, yeah, but I think she meant it in a gentle and loving way. She doesn't have the biggest vocabulary, but we manage to communicate." Thwack! "What are you laughing about? We *do* communicate."

"I bet. Anyway, you could probably use a little fashion upgrade."

"Oh, because you're so spiffy in your closetful of oversize sportswear?" Thwack!

I couldn't help noticing AJ had put a little something extra on that last pitch. "Hey, this isn't about me. You *asked* me what I thought. Anyway, just ask her to take you to the mall. Girls love taking their boyfriends shopping. It's well-known." Hehheh. It felt amazingly great to say that to *him*, for a change.

Thwack! "Maybe I'll try that," he said. "By the way, have you told your parents about your grandfather yet?"

See, it does totally suck when your significant other and your best pal are friends with each other, because then they can tag-team you. I shook out my throbbing hand, and said, "Can we try some off-speed stuff for a while? You, uh, don't want to burn yourself out too early."

"Good point. Just let me throw five more fast-balls, all right? Now, about that grandfather thing. You know your parents are totally going to notice eventually, right?"

Thwack! "Yeah, but —"

"And what if your grandfather hurts himself in the meantime?"

Thwack! "Well, I made him promise to call me if —"

"Dude. Listen to yourself. It's not your job to be responsible for him all day. You're not *his* grand-father; he's *yours*. Trust me, secrets suck. You'd feel so much better if you let this one go."

Thwack! *Wow,* I thought. *When did AJ suddenly start sounding logical?* "I'm working on it, all right?"

Thwack! "Like you're working on your throw-ing arm?"

Thwack! Without warning, AJ put everything he had into his last fastball. I barely got my glove up in time, and my hand felt like it was turning into hamburger meat. "What the hell was that?"

"Nothing. I'm just working out. *Somebody* has to be in shape for the season!"

"Don't worry about me," I said. "I'm doing what I have to do. Now, are we done for the day? My hand is killing."

He whipped his glove into the ball bucket and stormed off to his mother's office, where his little brothers were frolicking all over the copy machine. "Well," I muttered into the vast emptiness of the warehouse floor, "*that* went well."

I spent the whole stupid month worrying: What if my grandfather did fall or something? How was I supposed to tell AJ I could never play again without making him mad at me forever? And was Angelika tipping AJ off about stuff? Between all of that and getting ready for first-semester finals, I felt like I was in some kind of nightmarish, inescapable tunnel of stress. Plus, Angelika and I had to finalize the year-book layouts for all of the fall sports, and get as much done as we could for the winter ones. On the bright side, that meant we could squeeze in some time together between my visits to my grandfather, the workouts with AJ (which kept going even though AJ was being mighty touchy for a guy with a brand-new girlfriend), and the studying we both had to do.

There's nothing more romantic than working side by side with your partner by the warm, toasty glow of the computer monitor, judging, cutting, and pasting photos of other girls in skimpy uniforms. I mean, yes, we had to lay out all of the guys' sports, too. But guys at least wear some freaking clothing for most of their activities. And there isn't so much spandex involved. I was dying. And Angelika knew it.

The fun never stopped. If it wasn't the volleyball team, it was the gymnasts. Or the cheerleaders. The dance team. The cross-country girls in their ultra-short shorts. And Angelika kept asking, "So, do you think she looks pretty in this shot? Or how about this other girl? You don't think she's too, um, sweaty, do you?" I swear, the biggest relief of my life came when it was time to pick the shots for the golf team — thank God for nice, long khaki pants, I always say.

Naturally, Angelika gave me the hardest time over the swim team. It seemed like every third picture featured Linnie Vaughn, who was always smiling seductively, always dripping wet, and always wearing the smallest suits of any competitive swimmer in history. Angelika scrolled through everything we had with Linnie in it, and then stood up. She stuck out her hip in a supermodel pose and said, "Make me look beautiful! Darling, I am a star!" Then she strutted around the tiny office, repeating it. "Make me look beautiful! Make me look beautiful!" Then she bent down next to my ear and whispered, "Do *I* look that beautiful, Pete?"

"Not even close," I said. "She's just Linnie Vaughn. You're the most beautiful girl in the world!"

Apparently, that was the right answer.

Snap III

Nobody is around to take these pictures: They exist only in the mind of one young man, who sees them projected, over nights stretching into weeks, on the insides of his eyelids.

The first captures the loneliness of a snowy evening stretch of road. There are storefronts all along the far side of the street, shuttered now in advance of the dark and the snow that has already begun to fall in thick, side-blown sheets. Of course, a photo can't show the wind, but you know it is there in the bend of the scraggly road-side trees, the way the flakes seem to form slanted lines in the glow of the streetlight.

The next shows the same street, hours later. Now, the snow blankets everything, and falls in waves that are, if anything, drifting harder than before. You can see the patterns quite clearly as they are stabbed through by twin beams from the headlights of an unseen, approaching vehicle.

Frame three is all SUV. Blurred by snow, dark, and speed, the truck still shows up clearly enough that one can see its direction. If the painted lines on the road weren't buried, the car would be sliding across them at a slight angle. A fan of snow kicks up from behind one rear tire; the driver must have gunned the gas in an attempt to whipsaw his vehicle back in line.

That never works.

In frame four, the SUV is jammed up against what one assumes must be the curb. The driver, bathed in the glow of unseen red and blue lights, sits with his legs halfway out the door, staring straight into the lens without recognition.

18. a helping person

I was hanging out at my house with Angelika when the call came. It was the first week in February, right after exams ended. We were playing around on the couch, the snow was falling thickly outside, and Mom and Dad had both already called to say they were stuck in horrible snowstorm traffic on the highway. It was the kind of situation that's perfectly set up to make a guy ignore the phone.

In fact, a confession: I did ignore the phone, at first. Until the answering machine clicked in, and I heard Grampa saying, "Pick up the phone! I don't know who I am!"

Even in the panicky disentanglement of limbs that followed, I was already thinking: *Oh, God. He didn't say, "I don't know where I am"; he said, "I don't know* who *I am.*" I lunged for the phone, and amid the horrible squeals of feedback from talking with the handset too close to the machine, I said, "Don't hang up, Grampa! I'm here!"

The connection was terrible. It sounded like my grandfather was talking in some kind of distant, underground train tunnel. "Is Joan there?" he asked. Joan is the name of my dead grandmother.

"No, Grampa. She's, uh, well — she's not around. This is Peter."

"Who?"

"Your grandson. Peter!"

"Are you a helping person, Peter?" *A helping person?* I thought. *What the heck is a helping person?* There really ought to be a manual for these situations, but there isn't. Anyway, I made the lightning decision to be a helping person, whatever that was.

"Yes, Grampa, I am your helping person. Where are you?"

"I don't know. They moved the shoe store."

Holy cow. He was out in the storm. "Grampa, are you driving?"

"Yes. How else would I get to the shoe store?"

"Grampa, listen to me. Can you please pull over? Right now?"

"I can't. I need snowshoes. I couldn't find my snowshoes, so I . . . I don't know where I am. But I need the shoes."

Angelika could tell from my side of the convo that this was not a happy call. She squeezed my arm, and whispered, "Can I do something?"

I couldn't think. My grampa was out there in the dark, driving. "Listen to me," I said. "Just pull over, OK? I promise we'll get you some shoes tomorrow. All right?"

"Thank you. But I can't stop. I don't have any shoes. My feet are cold!"

Goose bumps rose all over my body. He was barefoot? Well, this was rapidly crossing over from "Grampa being Grampa," through "Please don't tell Mom," to "MAYDAY! MAYDAY!" I covered the phone with my free hand, and mouthed, "Call 9-1-1!" to Angelika. She dove for her purse and started fishing through it for her cell.

"All right," I said. "If you won't pull over, can you at least tell me where you are?"

"I'm not sure," he replied. "Everything looks so . . . different. But I might be near the interstate."

My heart skipped again. "Grampa, whatever you do, DON'T get on the highway, OK?"

"No highway," he said. "Got it. But why in the world would I get on the highway, young man? It's not like they sell shoes there."

"That's an excellent point, Gramp," I said.

Meanwhile, Angelika had dialed the police, and I heard her say, "We don't know where he is, but he's very confused. And he must be freezing. I don't think he has any shoes on."

"Oh, wait," Grampa said. "I just passed a sign."

I squeezed the handset so hard I thought it might crumble in my hand. "What did it say, Gramp? This is really important."

"It said STOP!" he whined. "But I'm not there yet."

"Gramp, I know you want to get some shoes, but can you slow down? Maybe if you can figure out what road you're on, I can help you figure out where the, uh, nice, warm shoes are."

Angelika whispered, "Can you find out where he is? Hurry! They want to send out a car!"

"Slow down? Really?" he said. "OK, if you say so. Ooh, look! That sign said 'bank.' I wonder if *I* go to that bank."

"I don't know. Can you tell me the name of the bank?"

"It's not one I've heard of, Pete. Pete, right? Anyway, it's . . . whoa, I skidded a little bit there. I think it's snowing. What were you saying?"

I could feel myself starting to cry. "The bank, Gramp. Tell me the name of the bank."

"It doesn't make sense. It's in some foreign language or something. Un-eye-vest? Uni-vest, maybe? What kind of name is *that* for a bank, anyway?"

"Univest?" I asked shakily. I knew where he was! "Grampa, is there a store with a big red picture of a target on your left?"

He didn't respond.

"Grampa, are you still there?"

"I'm having trouble controlling this thing. But yes, there's a big red target. Is that a shoe store? Because my feet are really —"

I dropped the house phone, grabbed Angelika's cell phone, and talked into it as fast as I could. When I thought back on it later, I realized I'd probably been shouting by that point. "He's in Quakertown, on Route 309. By the Target. In a gray Chevy. Please hurry!"

Angelika took back her cell, and I picked up our phone off the floor. Grampa was still babbling about shoes. I cut him off. "Grampa, are you cold all over?"

"Yes."

"Are you wearing a jacket?"

"I'm wearing a nice, warm robe. But it's snowing in here, and I can't close the window."

Well, that explained all the background noise. "What do you mean, you can't close the window?" I asked.

"There's no crank on it. I can't —"

"Grampa, listen. You need to pull over. Then we can work on getting the window shut. I can even help you turn up the heat in the car. Wouldn't that be good?" I felt like I was talking to a little kid. What was I going to do next, offer him a Fruit Roll-Up?

"Really? Are you sure I should? I still don't have shoes or anything."

"Trust me."

"What?"

"TRUST ME!"

"I can't hear you! There's a big noise here!" I heard it over my grandfather's voice, and even over the wind whistling through the open car window: a siren.

"PULL OVER!" I screamed.

"I — am — PULLING — OVER!" he screamed back. I looked at Angelika, who had clearly heard that outburst. I nodded in relief. She smiled, reached out, and squeezed my shoulder. But then, as the siren got louder, I heard a strange whistling and whooshing that sounded like an engine racing way too fast, followed by a long, long squeal of brakes and a surprisingly soft crunch.

"Grampa!" I yelped. "Grampa? Are you there? Are you OK?"

The wind sounds had stopped, but the siren was still wailing away, so I knew the phone was still working. I waited for what felt like minutes and minutes, with my heart pounding, my head resting on my hand, Angelika standing there not knowing what to do. Was my grandfather unconscious? Or, God forbid, dead? Was a police officer going to pick up the phone and ask me whether I was the next of kin? I heard some rustling, and realized my grandfather must have dropped the phone, then picked it up. "Hello?" he said. "Guess what? I think I pulled over!"

That was when I started to sob.

19. coming clean

They took Grampa to the hospital. I called both of my parents. My mom, who worked close to there, changed course to go meet the ambulance. Dad was coming from the opposite direction, so he came home and picked me up. After we dropped Angelika off at her house — she kissed me right in front of my father and made me promise to text when I knew anything — Dad and I were basically silent all the way to the emergency room.

The trip had seemed to take about a year and a half, especially in the snow, but when we arrived, Mom said my grandfather was still in the back area, getting X-rays. The doctors had said his body seemed to be perfectly fine, but that his ribs had whacked into the steering wheel, so they weren't taking any chances. As for his head, a neurologist had been called down, but Mom hadn't heard anything from her yet.

As soon as Mom had told us what little she knew, she asked me to tell her everything about Grampa's little excursion. I did, and then she surprised me. "I'm so proud of you," she said. "You did everything exactly right! The police officers told me how calm you and Angelika were, how you figured out where he was — all of it. My brave boy!"

Mom grabbed me around the waist, buried her head in my shoulder — I was startled to realize I was tall enough for that — and cried. Dad stood there awkwardly, alternately patting my shoulder and stroking Mom's hair. After a while, he said, "Yes, uh, great work, Peter." Which *had* to be the most enthusiastic thing he'd said to me in at least a year.

Too bad I didn't feel like I deserved the praise. "Mom, Dad," I said. A massive lump was forming somewhere behind my tonsils. I swallowed. "I have to tell you something. I . . . I . . . um, Grampa fell in October. And he's been forgetting more and more stuff. He keeps sticky notes posted all over his house to remind him of everything he has to do every day. I knew he was getting worse, and I . . ." Tears flowed down my face. "I didn't tell you. I mean, I tried last summer, but when Mom didn't believe me, I just gave up. But I should have said something. If Grampa dies, it's my fault!"

"Oh, Pete," Mom said between sniffles of her own, "this is *not* your fault. None of it's your fault."

She buried her face against my neck again and started weeping even harder. Dad started speaking: "Son, your mother is right. This is our responsibility. We knew your grandfather was having problems. We even made a deliberate decision to try and keep you from knowing how bad he was getting."

"Why, Dad? Why would you do that? I mean, Grampa's my —"

"I know, buddy. He's your favorite person. And we felt that, after all you'd been through with your arm, and starting high school on top of that . . . well, we thought you didn't need any additional stress."

Swell. That plan had worked out just perfectly — *not*.

Mom had gotten herself under control again, which was good, because if she had cried much more on me, I was pretty sure my shirt would have actually dissolved. "And, Pete," she said, "you have to understand. We knew things weren't right with your grampa, but we kept thinking we'd have more time before it got really bad. And if we need to move Grampa into an assisted living place . . . It's really expensive, so your father has been working overtime every chance he gets this whole year to try to save up some money for when the day comes that your grandfather can't live on his own anymore. But we should have told you a long time ago that this was going on. I'm so sorry you're finding out this way, Pete. I'm so sorry! But please believe me: We thought we were doing what was best for everyone."

Hmm, there had been a lot of that going around.

As things turned out, Grampa didn't have anything broken, but the neurologist wanted to keep him in the hospital overnight for a bunch of tests. They were transferring Grampa to a private room, so Mom decided to stay there and sleep in the chair. Dad and I would drive home through the storm before the roads became completely impassable. As we were getting ready to leave, the neurologist popped her head into the waiting room again, and it was almost like she could read our minds. She said, "By the way, I'd imagine you might be telling yourselves this was your fault, that you could have acted sooner and prevented it, yada yada. But dementia is a tricky thing, and it can seem pretty gradual until — boom! — the elderly person slips really, really quickly. We see this all the time, especially in close-knit families where the elderly person is very well loved. The hardest thing in the world for most of us is admitting when it's the end of an era."

Geez, AJ had been right again: Secrets *do* suck, and you *do* have to let go of them. If you don't, you can paralyze your whole life. Maybe somehow, underneath his Neanderthal exterior, he was more sensitive than I thought.

Grampa stayed in the hospital for two more days. The neurologist diagnosed him with Alzheimer's disease, and said it was probably time to move him into an assisted living place as soon as possible. Truthfully, I wasn't super-involved with the move, because I couldn't stand to see Grampa so unhappy, and because I was spending all my free time working with AJ, getting him ready for baseball tryouts. But Mom was telling me all about it, and I knew Grampa was pretty crushed.

With my usual luck, the tryouts for pitchers and Grampa's first day at the Gracewood Acres Assisted Living Community were only a day apart. The tryouts came first. I had come up with what I thought was the best possible plan for telling AJ I could never play again. It allowed me to keep working with him right up to the last minute, and it even gave me an excuse to be there for him during the actual event. I assigned myself to photograph the session for the school newspaper.

The tryouts were held in the gym right after school. I got there first, carrying my fastest long lens and my best camera body, all slung over my shoulder in Grampa's oldest leather camera bag — he had always called it his lucky bag, and I needed all the luck I could get. AJ came bounding into the locker room with his bat bag, sat next to me, and started putting on his cleats. "Oh, man, I am so pumped up, Pete! I feel great. I feel like I could throw ninety-five out there today. Whoever's catching better have, like, a steel-reinforced glove. Speaking of which, where's your equipment?"

I took a long, deep breath, and reached into my camera bag. I held up Numero Uno, and said, "Here's my equipment."

He just looked at me. And looked at me. And looked some more. Finally, he said, "You're not trying out?"

"AJ," I said, "I can't try out." Hoo boy, this was the hardest thing to say. "I, umm . . . well, the doctors didn't just say I *might* never pitch again. They said I *would* never pitch again. I wanted to tell you a million times, but I . . ." I couldn't even finish the sentence. Or look AJ in the eye.

"It's about freaking time you told me," he said.

"What do you mean?"

"Pete, I know I don't get straight As like you do, without even trying or anything. And I know I'm not always, like, all serious and solemn like you. But I'm not a moron. And I know when my best friend is full of crap about something. I've known it since we started throwing in December. Really, I think I've known it since the day you, um — the day you fell. But I kept waiting for you to tell me yourself."

I looked at AJ. He looked at me. "Um, AJ," I said, "I'm sorry. I really am. I was a complete moron."

AJ stood up and said, "Pete, I'm sorry, too. I know how much you wanted to play high school ball. Listen, if you want, I won't try out."

What? I thought. *Did he really just say that?*

"I'm serious. Just say the word. I mean, you're my catcher. You'll always be my catcher. I don't even know how to pitch with anybody else behind the plate. It probably wouldn't be any fun without you anyway."

I thought of everything I had overheard on the night of Linnie Vaughn's party: How lucky I was. How I had everything going for me except baseball. How much AJ *needed* to pitch. I stood up and grabbed AJ by the shirt. "Get your stuff on and get out there, AJ."

"Are you sure?"

"Dude, if you don't, I am going to give you *such* a beat-down."

He put a hand on my shoulder. "All right, Pete. If that's what you want." He reached down and started getting his other equipment out of his bag. "Hey, uh, are you still going to go out and watch? I mean, take pictures and stuff?" I nodded. "OK," he said. "Because I have one request."

"What is it?"

He struck a Linnie Vaughn pose and pointed at Numero Uno. "Make me look beautiful. Can you do that?"

"Dude," I said. "It's a camera, not a freaking magic wand!" He punched me in the good shoulder. Then he laughed, we grabbed our bags, and it was action time.

Not that I had any doubts, but AJ makes the team. Actually, if you want to know the truth, AJ *is* the team. All through the spring, I go to every single game. I'm really proud of my best friend. I mean, I'd

273

be lying if I said I never feel a stab of jealousy. But by the end of the season, I'm mostly just happy for him. It really hits me in the sixth inning of the last game of the playoffs. AJ is at bat, with guys on second and third. God, I wish I could be standing there on second base, waiting for AJ to drive me home like he's done a million times before. But I'm getting used to this, too.

Of course, there have to be two outs, and our team has to be losing by one run. It's only fitting that the whole season would come down to AJ with a bat in his hand, at what my old friend Henri Cartier-Bresson would call "the decisive moment." I'm crouched down behind the first base line, next to the dugout, with my camera trained on the exact spot where I know the next pitch is coming. I hold my breath so I won't shake the camera, push down the shutter button halfway, and wait. I press it the rest of the way just as AJ's bat connects, sending the ball way, way over the center fielder's head.

As everyone on our side of the stands goes bonkers, I take the camera away from my face, turn, and look into the crowd. I immediately spot Angelika, who is standing up with her fists in the air, between a shouting, jumping Elena and a bunch of camera gear. She sees me, and mouths, "Did you get the shot?"

I mouth back, "What do you think?" And I smile.

epilogue: fall, junior year

I walk into the lobby of the assisted living place and take a left by the elevators. My heart is pounding. I've visited my grandfather twice a week since he came here. Sometimes I bring AJ, when he's not too busy being the all-around athletic star of the school. Other times I bring Angelika. Grampa has a terrible memory for other people, but his face always lights up when he sees her. On this particular day, I'm alone, but I've brought a gift. On his good days, Grampa really likes it when I bring gifts. As I approach Grampa's room, I know this isn't going to be one of his good days. There have been fewer and fewer of those, anyhow. Mostly, Grampa just sits in the chair by the window, his legs covered with a ratty afghan, looking out over the back parking lot and the majestic Dumpster beyond. He was never much of a talker, it's true, but lately it's like there's a curtain separating him from the rest of the world.

The doctors say that soon, Grampa will forget how to speak altogether. Unless he refuses to eat before then, which would be the end. Or maybe he will lose his ability to swallow, and a little piece of food will lodge in his windpipe. Then he'll get pneumonia, which would also finish him off.

I try not to think about it.

Anyway, today he's talking, but I can't understand much of it. From what I can make out as I walk down the hallway, he's complaining to President Johnson about the way the Vietnam War is going. It's strange to hear these speeches he makes, because it's like he is magically transported back to the 1960s, when my Gram was alive, and my mom was a little kid. Mom says those were happy times in Grampa's life, so at least that's a plus.

I walk into the room, and he is looking right at me. His eyes are slow to focus, so I try to jog his memory. "Hi, Grampa!" I say, closing the distance and leaning over to give him a one-armed hug. The other arm is behind my back, holding Grampa's present. "It's me — Peter."

Grampa smells really clean whenever I visit. Mom says that means the home is taking good care of him. I guess so. "Peter?"

I nod.

"Are you my father, Peter?"

My eyes are burning. "No, I'm your grandson. Your father's name was Peter, too, but I'm your grandson."

He still looks completely puzzled. "Am I *your* father?"

Hoo boy. I shake my head. I hate this. I decide that maybe I should just show him what I've brought. If this doesn't get him focused, I don't know what will. I pull the little dinner tray table over so that it's right in front of Grampa's chair, and then lay the present on it. I ask him to help me rip off the wrapping paper, and he does. I notice that his hands are shaking. Mine are, too.

We get the paper off, and Grampa stares down at the framed photo I've brought him. It's an eagle, soaring, lit from below by the early morning rays of the sun at Hawk Mountain. Grampa traces one wing with his pointer finger, then the other. He slides his hand across the body of the bird, then looks at me with the fierce pride I haven't seen for months.

"I took this picture!" he exclaims.

"Well, no, Grampa. I took this picture. It was last week. I got up bright and early, like you always did. Mom drove me up there. I wanted to be there by sunrise, but I only have my learner's permit, so I couldn't drive until the sun came —"

"I took this picture!"

"Uh, anyway, I went to the mountain, and it was a perfect day: not too cold, but with the wind blowing in from the northwest. I sat down, set up your old tripod, and waited. And waited. And waited. I was about to give up and take the lens off the camera —"

Suddenly, Grampa leans forward and puts his hand on my arm. "The big lens? The four hundred?"

I'm excited. Grampa's here again, at least for a moment. He's really with me. "Yeah, the four hundred. I had it stopped down to f-eleven because the sun was getting pretty bright. Anyway, that was when I saw her."

"Her?"

"The eagle. She came over the ridge maybe a hundred feet away from me. I mean, she was so close I had to zoom out. I mean, I almost could have gotten her with a medium-wide lens. It was like she was posing or something."

"And then?"

"And then I did just what you always said. I got her in the viewfinder, breathed deep, pressed the button halfway, tracked her for a second or so, and then shot fifteen frames in burst mode. That was it. She flew back across the ridge, and that was the end of it. But I knew I had the shot. You don't think it's underexposed, do you? I mean, I could try to fix it up in Photoshop if you think it's too washed-out or —"

Grampa squeezes my arm again. He leans so close I feel his breath on my forehead. "Peter, it's perfect!" Then he sits up straight just as one of the aides comes in with his lunch. He calls her over and gestures at the picture. She says, in that slightly patronizing tone they all use in the locked ward, "What is it, Mr. Goldberg?"

He looks at her and puts on his biggest, warmest grin. "It's an eagle, miss. I took that picture!"

She smiles professionally, and says, "It's very nice, Mr. Goldberg. Now, where can I put this delicious food I've brought for you?"

Grampa looks at me, and his face is clouded, uncertain again. "I did take that picture. Right? With my 1949 Ciro-Flex Three-Point-Five camera! Didn't I, Dad?"

My breath comes out in a whoosh. Behind me, the aide fluffs Grampa's pillows, and walks out of the room. I take Grampa's hand and squeeze. "Yes, you did take that picture. Great job!"

I make it out to the hallway before the sobs overtake me. My back slides down the wall of the corridor until I am squatting with my head in my hands. I don't know how much time passes before my breath calms down again, but eventually I wipe my face on my sleeve. That's when I realize Grampa is talking to himself. Maybe because my head is against the wall, I can hear him perfectly. He is saying the same thing over and over, in tones of little-boy wonder:

"I got the shot, Dad. I got the shot!"

Eventually, I get myself cleaned up and walk down the hall to the elevator. When I walk out of the nursing home, with my camera dangling from my neck, AJ, Angelika, and Elena Zubritskaya are leaning against the side of my car, waiting for me. I had told Angelika I wanted to visit my grandfather alone; giving him the eagle had felt like it should be a private ceremony. But I guess she had figured out I might need some support right afterward.

"Dude!" AJ shouts when I am still twenty feet away. "Did you bestow the bird?" He hasn't developed a more sensitive manner of speaking over the years, but he's here for me — and I am feeling the love.

Angelika elbows him in the ribs, and says, "What Adam means to say is —"

"I know. I know. Yes, the bird has been bestowed."
Angelika and Elena both smile, and AJ puts one arm
around each of them. As AJ gives me a double
thumbs-up, I grab my camera and swing it up to capture the moment. Looking through the viewfinder, I
can tell this shot is going to be a keeper, the kind of
picture you look at years and years into the future.

I press the button halfway down, and everything
springs into focus: Angelika is looking right at me,
laughing with AJ, but also concerned. AJ has the
exact same smirk he's always had, but his eyes are
searching my face, too. Elena is tucked in under
AJ's shoulder, beaming up at him. If you had told
me freshman year that my hound dog best friend
would fall deeply in love with his very first girlfriend
and bond with her forever, I'd have laughed — but
there it is.

I flash back for an instant to my grampa, and wonder whether I should have corrected him, should
have told him again that I had taken the picture of
the eagle. But, I realize, in a bigger sense, that picture *was* his all along. He took me to the mountain,

he gave me the tools, he gave me the love. I just put myself in the right place, at the right time, and got the shot.

Back in the present, AJ, Angelika, and Elena fill the frame. I press the button.

It's funny. You'd think I'd be in a rush to get home, check out the picture on my computer, find out whether it's really as perfect as I think it will be. But I don't need to check.

Grampa was right: Sometimes, you just know it when you see it.

about the author

Jordan Sonnenblick is the author of the acclaimed *Drums, Girls & Dangerous Pie*; *Notes from the Midnight Driver*; *Zen and the Art of Faking It*; and the 2011 Schneider Family Book Award Winner *After Ever After*. He lives in Bethlehem, Pennsylvania, with his wife and two children.

this is teen

Want to find more books, authors, and readers to connect with?

Interact with friends and favorite authors, participate in weekly author Q&As, check out event listings, try the book finder, and more!

Join the new social experience at
www.facebook.com/thisisteen